The Accidental Philanderer

The Accidental Philanderer

Dennis McKay

iUniverse®

THE ACCIDENTAL PHILANDERER

iUniverse books may be ordered through booksellers or by contacting:

iUniverse
1663 Liberty Drive
Bloomington, IN 47403
www.iuniverse.com
1-800-Authors (1-800-288-4677)

ISBN: 978-1-4917-8177-7 (sc)
ISBN: 978-1-4917-8178-4 (e)

Library of Congress Control Number: 2015919014

Print information available on the last page.

iUniverse rev. date: 12/07/2015

Chapter 1

Over a rise at the far end of the cemetery, a line of trees flushed in brilliant hues of red and gold met an azure horizon with stunning clarity. Mourners stood near a hardwood casket resting on a steel stand at a freshly dug grave. "It is a fine piece of craftsmanship with the proper religious connotations," the funeral home director had told Niels Pettigrew, recommending the casket for his wife. It was adorned with a nameplate on the interior panel—*Laura Pettigrew, 1959–2010*—and six silver handles attached to silver-plated hinges, each with an etching of *The Last Supper.* They reminded Niels of upscale but utilitarian door knockers as a vague thought filtered in his mind: these knockers would get no answer.

The squeaky iterations of a wren rising in volume and pitch and ending in a rapid cascade of tweets caught Niels's ear over the reverend's drone. "Laura, a generous contributor to church functions and projects, staunch member of MADD, dutiful Christian, and faithful wife and mother …"

Finally, Reverend Pritchard, a lank of a man floating a prominent Adam's apple above his clerical collar, offered a closing prayer that Niels heard but didn't hear.

The distinct bubbling chatter of the little wren coming from a line of trees along a gravel lane had drowned out every noise, even the condolences of people passing by. It seemed a perfect song for such an occasion—ethereal, as though sung specifically for the recent widower.

Andrea stood at her father's side in a slack-jawed daze, an expression she had worn ever since Niels's call that her mother had died in an airplane crash en route to Minnesota, of all places, to attend a MADD conference, of all things. "Dad," she whispered. "Dad?"

Niels leaned his head toward the sound of his daughter's voice until the little wren was no longer audible. The absent part of his mind wanted to see the little songbird before he returned to the obligation at hand. He looked into his daughter's eyes—her mother's eyes, everyone had always said. But there was something in Andrea's gaze that her mother had never possessed. Even in this terrible moment, there was a gleam like a shiny brown glow. She revealed a sensitivity of concern, unlike Laura's squinting slant of uncertainty, which had seemed as though she was always searching for defects. "Yes, Andrea," he said. "Yes, dear."

"We need to get home." She pursed her lips in a nervous puck, drawing her eyebrows together over the bridge of her slender, delicate nose.

"Ah, yes," Niels said as he realized there was one more hurdle. "The reception."

Laura's heirloom double-pedestal dining table, in all its extended-leaf glory, occupied the middle of the dining room and was covered by an embroidered tablecloth, a stack of white china set at one end and cutlery pocket-folded in cloth napkins at the other. There were bowls of shrimp wrapped in bacon, platters of fresh fruit sliced in an array of colors, pinwheel sandwiches on tiered plates, and cookies and other desserts, all of it so very nice. Laura would have been pleased. On a side table, much to Niels's surprise, a bar had been set up with wine and an ice-filled beverage tub of bottled beer.

It was a sedate gathering with a cluster of soft conversations among guests as they lingered over glasses of wine or sipped on beers, while Niels gripped an eight-ounce bottle of Perrier almost as a prop.

Because of Laura's stringent policy of departing social gatherings serving alcohol at the first sign of *discord*, such as slurred words or even an uproar of laughter, Niels habitually had felt uneasy, as though he was not one of them—the imbibers. At any moment, he could receive the tight-lipped squint, a look that meant he should go immediately to the closet, retrieve their coats, and offer a quick thank-you before they would depart.

A neighbor had arranged the caterer, and Niels hadn't known they were serving alcohol. Laura would not have approved. In fact, he figured she may well be turning over in her grave. She considered liquor to serve no purpose other than putting people in situations that they would later regret.

The day seemed surreal, like an out-of-body experience, as Niels watched and listened, his corporeal being navigating its way among various clusters of people. He saw himself, Niels Pettigrew, a tall, wide-shouldered man with a general heaviness to his face and body that had softened his chiseled features of youth to those of a paunchy middle-aged businessman. More accurately, not youth but rather young adulthood, for he had been an average-looking, somewhat nerdy boy, shy and unassuming, who, growing up, had experienced two childhoods.

The first had been in Lower Merion, a well-to-do Philadelphia neighborhood with all the accoutrements—family membership in a country club, vacations at the family beach house on the Jersey Shore, and a tony private elementary school. A gifted student with a keen aptitude for numbers, Niels had been a happy boy with some like-minded friends who enjoyed collecting stamps and coins.

But by the time Niels was nine, his father had squandered his inheritance on a string of business fiascos and died when he drove his car off a cliff. It was ruled an accident, but there were whispers.

He and his mother's lives had abruptly changed from those of affluence in a Main Line residence to those of subsiding on a limited stipend from a life insurance policy in a two-bedroom rambler. Niels's new school was public, and his classmates were a rough lot with blue-collar pedigrees and penchants for settling disagreements with their fists.

At first Niels was the subject of bullying until the antagonizers tired of it, and he became like a piece furniture in the classroom, never speaking unless the teacher called his name and always making his answers as short as possible, never trying to show off his intellect.

An academic scholarship, including room and board, to his father's prestigious prep school in Connecticut arrived too late to save Niels socially, for he had grown into a withdrawn boy. He did, however, make a few acquaintances in the nature club, where his interest in birding flourished.

And then came the growth spurt his senior year that honed the round face into a sweep of high cheekbones that set his eyes like twin blue stars, and he had a body that was suddenly tall, lithe, and lean—a handsome lad who, much to his fluster, drew the attention of the opposite sex when he entered college.

But it had been a short-lived, uncomfortable beauty that began to fade by thirty. He was a man more at ease as Clark Kent than Superman. Still, if one looked closely, some of the beauty, not completely buried by excess, remained in the noble contour of the face and slate-blue eyes fringed by long, curving lashes that he hid behind a pair of thick-lens, horn-rimmed glasses, which he absentmindedly pushed back up the bridge of his nose with his index finger as he conversed with neighbors.

Shuffling on to fellow members from the Buck's County Audubon bird-watching club, Niels attempted to stay reasonably upbeat before he drifted on to consoling members from their nondenominational church. He could almost hear Laura saying, "Our type of people, Niels." She had a habit of ending her comments to her husband with his name.

It was a challenge to keep a stiff upper lip and carry on, and by day's end, Niels was exhausted with fatigue he had never experienced before—a bone-weary tiredness with a woozy sense of instability. He felt adrift, as if the rudder to this life were no longer there.

Finally, the last guest departed, and Niels plopped down on the sofa in the family room that Laura had immaculately decorated in a wildlife motif that complemented her Main Line ambience of adaptive reuse.

Andrea sat in her mother's sleigh-seat mahogany sewing chair, which Laura had painstakingly restored. She raised her head and stared vacantly at her father as the finality of the moment took hold. Her relationship with Laura had been somewhat unusual in its formality. Andrea had always called her Mother, not that Niels remembered Laura insisting on it, but as a young child, Andrea had intuited from her mother's stiff, bristly manner that it was the proper designation. Niels couldn't fathom Laura being called Mom. It did not fit. Everything about her, from her straight-backed carriage to her slightly nasal, nose-up-in-the-air accent, said "Mother." Their relationship had been more like that of mentor with a gifted prodigy. Nonetheless, they had been close.

Niels slipped off his black dress shoes, and without thinking, he eased his feet up on the ship's table that Laura had bought at an estate sale in Bryn Mawr years ago.

The distinct shrill of his wife's voice waffled in the recesses of his mind with its haughty emphasis on selected words. "It's gauche," the ghostly voice said, drawing out the second syllable, *go-shhh*, "for one to put his feet on the table. Remove them at once, Niels."

Niels started to lift his feet from the table and caught himself. He glanced about the room, which was permeated with his wife's influence. A replica of a bird nest with three speckled eggs rested on the table next to his crossed feet, a framed picture of Laura and Niels birding in the Florida Everglades was stationed on the French Provincial hutch in the corner, which Laura had refinished with chalk paint, and the needlepoint of an American eagle hung over the gas fireplace. But his wife's scent, which had lingered over the house like a musty mist, had disappeared from the premises as though her essence had departed along with her in death.

He looked at Andrea, her eyes squinted to puffy slits, but in her gaze there was resiliency, a willingness to carry on. "Your mother had arranged a trip for next week to Barcelona to celebrate our twenty-fifth anniversary." Niels removed his glasses and rubbed his eyes with the heels of his hands.

Andrea appeared a shadowy image, like some amorphous entity. He put the glasses back on, refocused, and saw his daughter with a question in her eyes.

"Oh, yes, Mother had told me about bird-watching in …" She threw her hand in the air, trying to remember the name.

"Ebro Delta." Niels heard the longing in his voice. He raised his chin in the general direction of an envelope on the mantel. "She secured a great deal a few months back on airfare," he said as he turned his gaze back to his daughter.

"You should go, Dad." Andrea nodded as if to make a point. "Airfare has shot up. I bet you could sell the second ticket for a nice profit." The pragmatic business side of Andrea was coming out. She had recently passed her CPA exams and was a rising star at an international law firm in the city. She had her father's acumen for mathematics.

"No, they're nontransferable."

"The airlines should refund you for Mother's ticket." Andrea leaned forward and nodded her head, her brow furrowed. "Bereavement," she said.

"I'll consider it," Niels said as he looked at the picture of himself and Laura on the hutch. A pair of binoculars hung on Niels's neck, and there was a look of stardust in his eyes, while in Laura's gaze—try as she might to smile—there still remained that constant slant of appraisal.

He remembered how wonderful he felt at that moment, for earlier they had spotted a Cuban pewee, a very rare bird from the flycatcher family. Laura saw it first, and Niels honed in with his binoculars. When he saw the white crescent behind its eye, his heart seemed to stop for a moment before he heard its distinctive call, *dee-dee-dee*. Laura raised her camera to snap a picture, but the bird disappeared into a thicket of mangroves. But what a moment it had been. Even Laura had commented that it was special.

"Dad, you should go to Europe. Mother told me how much you were looking forward to bird-watching over there."

"Andrea, I don't know, dear."

"Dad," Andrea said as though she were the parent, "you'll regret if you don't."

* * *

The week before departure, Niels spent time at his office, clearing his slate as executive VP and managing director for a major insurance company. Swift analysis had been his forte in the complex world of risk and uncertainty—a world he understood with his keen mind for numbers and probability. However, in regard to the recent changes in his personal life, he had no answer or comprehension of the risk that lay ahead.

Since Laura's passing, Niels often had to ask people to repeat what they had just said, as his mind seemed off-kilter, as though his internal gyroscope were readjusting, and on a couple of occasions, he forgot where he was. Once he got lost on the way home from work, and another time he got off on the wrong floor at his high-rise office building. On that occasion he became completely befuddled before he realized his mistake.

Staying busy helped him from wobbling completely off course from the orbit that Laura had designed and regulated. He had been eating cold leftovers. He didn't know how to cook. He didn't have a clue about shopping for groceries or where to go to pick up laundry or any of the other multitudes of chores that Laura had handled.

Anyway, he thought a change of scenery might help his situation, especially at an expensive hotel with room service, a concierge, cleaners, and all the other amenities that might help him get back in his orbit—or at least find a new one.

* * *

The flight from Philadelphia to Barcelona was an eight-hour nonstop one. Big-boned and standing more than six foot three in his stocking feet, Niels was now relieved that Laura, not wanting him cramped for such a long flight, had insisted that they sit in business class.

He had always flown first-class or business for his job. An actuary by trade, he had risen through the ranks at his firm to his current position. A master at simplifying actuarial minutia, he flew out from time to time to consult and answer questions at regional offices. But on personal trips he had always paid economy, and unless he got a seat facing the bulkhead, he squeezed in. And Lord help him if someone of girth took the seat next to him.

Niels settled into his window seat. The middle one would have been Laura's. This was his first flight since her plane crash—the cause of which, he had learned, was most likely due to wind shear. He didn't have a fear of flying, for the probability of someone's plane crashing two weeks after their spouse's was astronomical.

He could almost see her sitting next to him in her brown pleated skirt and white blouse with the frilly collar. She would have picked out his travel attire—gray herringbone sport coat, light blue Brook Brothers shirt with starch in the collar, and laundered gray slacks.

But Niels had never been to the cleaners. It seemed out of his orbit. Instead he wore a polo shirt and Dockers that he had run through the washing machine and dryer—a first. It had taken him fifteen minutes and a few false starts before he figured out how to run the washer.

A wave of uncertainty swept over him as he wondered why he had ever agreed to embark on this trip by himself. He was a dependent man—his controlling wife at home and the corporate machinery at work that scheduled his business trips, airlines, rental cars, and hotels. Barely functioning at home, how would he ever navigate by himself in Spain without his domestic manager?

But here he was, safely ensconced in his seat, his luggage stowed in the cargo bin. There was no turning back. He turned his attention to a swarm of passengers bustling onboard. Most were in a hurry, and many were tense. But flying was second nature to Niels.

His motto was "Travel light, arrive early." He enjoyed observing the people board the plane and comparing them to birds. The petite women with her brown hair in a bun brought to mind a sparrow. A tall gawky man, a heron.

His attention was drawn to a woman in a finely cut pantsuit coming down the aisle. Tall and dark-haired with an insouciant Euro air, she wore dangling gold hoop earrings, and her big brown eyes were alert like a bird of prey. There was something wild and dangerous in her manner as if she lived by her own set of rules.

The flow of traffic stopped. An elderly woman needed assistance with stowing her carry-on in the overhead. Niels removed his glasses and wiped them with a tissue in preparation for some reading he had brought. As he put them back on, he felt a presence as people get from time to time when they sense someone is watching them. But even more, there was something uncanny and strong as if it was being transmitted on a higher frequency.

When he looked up, there *she* was standing at his row of seats, staring point-blank at him. *Oh my God, what a look.* He felt a quiver shoot down his spine as her bold gaze seemed to take him into some otherworldly place, a forbidden place where he had never treaded and had never considered going to.

She looked up at the seat number below the baggage bin as a knowing smile flickered across her face. She slid over and sat next to Niels. "Ha … loo," she said in a voice with a distinct echo of Spain.

He nodded hello and turned his attention to a canvas satchel on his lap that contained a birder magazine, a *New York Times* Sunday crossword, and a hardback book. He felt her eyes on him as he fumbled nervously for the book, but he finally got it out and stowed the rest under his seat.

"There is magic in the air."

Startled, Niels turned to the woman. On her face was a look of bemused interest as if she had known him for years, as if they were old friends. "I beg your pardon."

"Bar … ce … lo … na," she said, drawing out the syllables. "Our destination is magic in the autumn." Even in a sitting position, her entire figure had a restless, insatiable energy, as if her body emitted a hum.

"Ahh," Niels said, turning back to his book, a biography of John Muir. Again he sensed her gaze on him and tried to ignore it, but her presence was undeniable and disconcerting. Feeling cornered and trapped, he dared not look at her, and he opened to the prologue.

Without warning, her hand came into his purview and settled on his forearm, her touch confident and warm on his bare skin. A strain of fear and arousal registered in him like a cannon shot.

"You must come with me to Aristo's party tonight," she said.

It dawned on Niels that this crazy woman was sitting in the seat intended for his wife. "I do not know anyone by the name of Aristo," he said as he turned back to the woman, "and I do not know you, madam."

"Hah," she said in a challenging tone before the flight attendant interrupted to ask her to bring her seat forward.

Niels felt like screaming for help. What did this woman want of him? And what had she set off that seemed to have frayed his already wobbling orbit dangerously close to another galaxy.

She straightened her seat and said to Niels, "You need to come. It will be so grand with so many interesting artists from Barcelona in attendance."

"I must say no."

She began to speak, and he raised his hand. "No. No."

He turned his attention to his book, but from the corner of his eye, Niels saw a man in a business suit take the aisle seat. He hoped—oh, how he hoped—that she would turn her attention to him.

She glanced at the man to her left and then leaned over toward Niels, her arm against his.

"It is a long flight, Paco."

Indeed, Niels thought, *this was going to be a long flight. A very long flight, indeed.*

Chapter 2

During takeoff the woman had clamped her fingers onto Niels thigh. There was a desperateness in her touch that kept him from attempting to remove it, and he didn't want a scene either. Who knew what she might do or say, so he left it there, her leaning tight against him. When the plane leveled off, she loosened her grip, and Niels removed her hand and put it on the armrest, not looking at her, hoping for the best.

"I get a little panicky during the takeoff," she said to Niels in a confidential voice, "but I am fine now."

Niels felt like asking about her definition of *fine*, but instead he only nodded, keeping his eyes on chapter 1. He admired John Muir's unwavering activism for preservation of the wilderness.

Laura had pointed out that Muir had dismissed organized religion as a young man. "Christian fundamentalism no less," she had said. But Niels countered that the great man's place of worship was the mountains and nature. "That is no excuse for ignoring the Sabbath," his wife replied with a taint of scorn in her tone. He had wanted to respond that there was more than one way to skin a cat, but he kept it to himself. It was easier that way, just as attending church every Sunday was too. Laura was subtle in getting her way—a look of expectation that Niels could not disappoint, a tone in her voice that said, "I know you believe as I do on this, Niels."

Furthermore, John Muir was a righteous man who had lived an exemplary life. Was it so terrible to avoid Sunday services when the rest of your life was far more Christian than most regular attendees? Sometimes in a moment of mind-wandering, Niels thought about what it would be like to go off in the wilderness like Muir and live a simple existence for months on end.

The woman leaned her shoulder into Niels. "Paco, you should consider contact lens and allow your hair to grow out."

On occasion, Niels still received unwanted attention from women who saw remnants of his youthful good looks. He wondered for an instant if this uncomfortable situation would be occurring had he not removed his glasses just when she had first encountered him. If he had left them on, she more than likely would have looked at him as the uninteresting man he considered himself to be—a nerdy, overweight actuary who enjoyed the solitude of birding.

He slammed the book shut and grabbed the frames of his glasses as if to secure them on his nose and turned to face his antagonist. "Look," he said in a raised voice that drew the attention of the man in the aisle seat. Niels exchanged a "help me" look with the man who turned quickly back to his laptop as if to say, "She's all yours." In a lowered voice, he said, "Please, madam, leave me alone. Please."

"Paco—"

"This is not who I am," Niels said as he removed his glasses and stared at her with myopic vacancy. He put the glasses back on and said through a clenched jaw, "This is who I am."

"No, it is not," she said in a voice of subtle determination, "it is a mask you wear."

Not only her words but the manner in which she delivered them struck a chord in Niels like a bell alerting him to the truth she had spoken. Walls were beginning to crumble. "What is it you want of me?"

She extended her long arm and put her long finger with a perfectly manicured nail on top of Niels's book. She pointed to the

he said as a segment of his mind listened to the thrum of the jet engines vibrating like minor shock therapy.

After a momentary silence, she said, "I am an artist. My grandmother taught me, and she learned from Picasso." Her tone was matter-of-fact as if this were no big deal.

"Pablo Picasso?"

"Yes, Paco, the great Picasso." She brought her fist under her chin, elbow resting on the armrest. "They were lovers when Nana was a young woman." Her eyebrows flared up, and her gaze was that of a ribald earth mother. "She often said he was a better lover than artist. Hah," she blurted out. "How do you like that?"

"Fascinating," Niels said.

"I am Nina de la Cerda." She drew her surname out, emphasizing each syllable. *De. La. Cer. Da.* She removed her hand from her chin, reached for his hand, and laced her fingers in his.

Her touch shot a surge through Niels like an electric current. Part of him wanted to pull away, but another—a stronger part that was unknown to him until this moment—squeezed her hand.

There was something comforting about being in an airplane twenty-five thousand feet above the earth with Nina at his side. It seemed as though he could forget what had recently transpired in his life, high above the land where all his problems existed, and let himself relax as though he were leaving one life and landing in a new one.

She went on to tell of her parents' marriage, which had lasted all of three years. "My grandmother told me they were like fire and ice, always at each other." Nina promised herself never to marry. She wanted "to meet life as it comes to me, and when I see one who interests me."

Her figure was angular and strong as though it held much in reserve, and her tone maintained a reasonable resonance as she continued on as though she didn't have to win him over anymore. She had him, and they both knew it. There was a hauntingly dark beauty about her. It was as if behind the madness there was a deep, dark secret she was hiding from.

* * *

At a taxi queue outside the Aeroport de Barcelona, Nina and Niels stood waiting. Behind them the terminal's control tower was shaped like a flying saucer attached to a spiral tower of steel and glass. Glass was everywhere at this airport—colored glass in the ceilings of the terminal, tables of glass in the departure areas, continuous glass walls that allowed natural light to flood into all the public spaces. It was sleek and shiny and so very modern that it seemed to Niels as though he had walked through the looking glass into another world.

Nina scanned past a line of black-and-yellow taxis up the airport entrance road. "My friend, the Count, should be arriving any minute to pick us up in his limo," she said as she shielded her eyes from the afternoon sun.

The limousine was no such thing. It was an old, dinged, and dented Audi driven by a scruffy fellow dressed in a tee shirt and cutoffs, a cigarette dangling from his lip. Nina embraced the man as though he were a long-lost brother. "Enrico, mi amigo."

There was a similar crazy gaze to this unshaven Spaniard. He was somewhere in his thirties with a three-day growth of stubble. "Nina, mi amor," he said as he stood back from her, hands on her shoulders, a pirate's gleam in his eyes. He reached into his shirt pocket for his cigarettes and offered her one.

She smiled with a reckless air as if this ignoble character had let loose something inside her. "No," she said, waving her hand, "deje." She tilted her head toward Niels. "This is Paco," she said, "he is coming to the fiesta tonight." Her tone was that of one who had caught a big prize to exhibit.

"Ahhh," Enrico said as he shook a finger at Nina, his eyes shining mischief.

Enrico was a stump of a man, built like a laborer with thick arms and shoulders, and a thicket of black wavy hair added to his scoundrel image. He stared up at Niels as if he was studying a work of art, the darting eyes looking him over from head to toe. "Hombre grande," he said through a grin. He bowed and waved his hand toward his vehicle. "After you, señor," he said in an overly dramatic Spanish accent.

The car pulled away from Barcelona Airport with Nina and Niels in the backseat. Niels had slept not a wink on the flight as Nina had talked constantly about a wide range of subjects from World Cup soccer to the Spanish Civil War. She was obviously well educated and smart in a crazy fox sort of way.

The jet lag gnawed at Niels as he tried to keep his eyes open while Nina jabbered away in Spanish to Enrico, who nodded and looked at her in the rearview mirror. He only occasionally turned his attention to the highway traffic, the sound of which, though heavy, had a softer hum than the bigger American cars, bringing home the fact that he was far from Philadelphia.

Niels felt himself drifting off and sat up. He did not want to fall asleep in the company of these two.

Nina leaned forward, hand on the top of the driver's seat, and spoke softly to Enrico, who turned his head and offered a smile, revealing large, irregular teeth that seemed capable of breaking an iron rod in two with a snap of his muscular jaw.

Niels's antennae told him that Nina had something up her sleeve. Was he a pawn in some game Nina and her artist friends enjoyed playing on total strangers? Or was he some prize to be shown off? *Look what I have found—a grieving Americano widower. He is a big one, no?* Part of Niels wanted to get out of the car and find his own way to his hotel and be done with these unpredictable characters. But Nina had stirred something in him that he never knew existed or that possibly had not existed prior to Laura's death. Where it came from or what it was, he did not know. He only knew that something about him was different.

It was triggered during the plane flight with Nina, as his imaginary wall had come down, offering a new view to this life. He remembered the moment it had occurred, when she laced her fingers in his. Never had he felt such a charge of arousal. It seemed to have broken off something from his protective armor. Not that he was going to do anything out of the norm with his moral compass, but maybe he would let his ship sail where the wind took him and observe. Like a good birder in an exotic jungle, he would pay careful attention to Nina and her associates and people-watch.

He imagined that they were a unique lot of characters. So what harm would a night in a foreign land with Nina and her friends do him? An American bachelor in Spain? My goodness, he was a single man now. Things had changed. His life would forever be different from before, just as Nina had told him. "Out of tragedy comes a new paradigm." *Tonight*, Niels thought, *it would begin.*

The car swerved sharply to the left, and consequently Niels leaned into Nina. She turned to him, her brow raised as if a grand idea had just come over. "Paco, you get some rest at your hotel, and we will pick you up at five for Aristo's fiesta."

Niels turned his attention to the front of the car as Enrico weaved in and out of cars, zipping along like a Grand Prix driver. Niels took off his glasses. It was better to see only the blur of traffic. "I didn't think anything began in Spain until much later."

"That is true." Nina paused and then said, "You really are better looking without those old-fashioned glasses."

He felt a blush in his cheeks, but this time Niels wasn't upset. "Why the early time?"

"It is an old tradition on the estate to have an early party after the harvest. There is no longer a harvest, but Aristo is always looking for an excuse for a fiesta," Nina said and laughed.

At the front desk to the four-star hotel that Laura had reserved, Niels waited in line to register. The place had been a palace in the nineteen century, and it had been converted in 1945. Laura had done research online to find a hotel located in the heart of the city's historic district. El Hotel Catalán combined old world and modern with granite steps and a hand-carved mahogany railing that led to the second floor. These details were in contrast to the sleek utilitarian sofas and low glass tables in the lobby.

The hotel was bustling with people, and Laura had said that this was the last big week of tourists and vacationers.

Niels told the clerk his name. "One moment, sir." The man, who was in his early twenties, typed into his computer, and his smiling face soon turned to a frown. "A problem, sir."

"Yes," Niels said as he sensed a snafu.

"Your reservation is not until tomorrow."

There was no corporate assistant to call or competent wife to deal with this. He was alone. "That is not possible." There was no way Laura, who was efficient to a fault, would have made a mistake.

The clerk checked his computer screen. "Today was canceled."

"What? When?"

Again the young man scanned his screen. "It seems," he said and then looked up, "ten minutes ago." The man shrugged as though to say it is out of my hands. "It was taken immediately."

"What," Niels exclaimed. *My God*, he thought, *Nina.*

"Is there someone you can stay with? I am afraid all the hotels are booked."

A sudden wave of fatigue came over Niels as he wished he had never decided to make this trip alone. If Laura had been here, this would not have happened, and then his thought was tempered by the fact that if his wife had been here, he would never have met Nina. His mind seemed to be spinning out of control as if he didn't know what to think anymore, how to think. He was too spent with jet lag to explain that a crazy woman had sabotaged his schedule. "Is there a restroom I can freshen up in?"

A frown came over the clerk. "Sir?" He did not understand the question.

"May I leave my bags here until tomorrow?"

The clerk smiled. "Of course, sir," he said as he motioned for a bellhop.

After Niels washed his face in the men's room in the hotel restaurant, he took a seat in a tall leather chair in a nook off the lobby. A bookshelf with glass cabinet doors ran along the back wall that brought to mind a reading room. Niels checked his watch. There were three hours before Nina and Enrico were supposed to pick him up.

Away from Nina's influence, a sense of despair came over Niels. He did not have a room for the night, and if she did not show, which was a possibility, he could end up spending the night on a park bench. And if she did show, would he really go off with her? How could he trust her after his room had been canceled? The fatigue of the flight and the general uncertainty if this trip were a wise choice weakened his resolve about starting things over. *New paradigm, indeed.*

He wished that Laura were here with him. If she were, they would be napping right now in their room. And later they would walk about the city, getting their bearings, and then they'd have an early dinner at some quaint restaurant that Laura would have found online. His old orbit that his wife had regulated with drill sergeant efficiency seemed very appealing at the moment. But she was dead, and Niels was alive. And he told himself he must try to make the best of it.

It was strange that his next option without Laura was Nina, and then it dawned on him that he had no other options. Even with all of her shenanigans, she had ignited a spark of desire that would not extinguish. It was something foreign and a bit scary and the likes of which he had never experienced. He decided to let the events of the day come as they may. He sat back and began chapter 1 of the Muir book.

It was no use. He could not concentrate on reading. He told himself it was jet lag, and he decided to rest for a bit. But there was a restlessness ransacking his body, as if he had been invaded by a foreign entity.

This was unusual, for Niels had always had a capacity to catnap in any sort of situation. On trains, on planes, or in the backseat of a car, he could cross his arms against his chest, tuck his chin into his neck, and drift off.

He tried to dismiss the thought that Nina was the cause of his internal unrest or that he was actually looking forward to the gathering this evening. "It is what it is," he told himself as he closed his eyes and hoped for the best.

At ten to five, Niels woke from an unsettled nap and went out front to wait for his ride.

Outside the hotel the clanging gongs of tower bells drew Niels attention down the street to the Barcelona Cathedral, a grand stone structure adorned in spires and arches. The gonging sound echoed in his mind as a heightened sense of awareness came over him. When the bells stopped, a shudder ran through him, forwarding himself to somewhere faraway before the city hum of traffic and people coming and going snapped him back to the present.

He expected his ride would be late, and there was a gnawing sense that it was possible they would not show. The thought of it made him sad. Then he would have been deserted and left alone in Barcelona to fend for himself.

At 5:40 p.m., feeling abandoned, he returned to his chair in the corner room. He would need to eat soon, maybe go out and find a restaurant. Then he could—

"Paco!"

Chapter 3

Aristo's house was on a sprawling estate that appeared to have seen its glory days decades ago. As they drove past the crumbling brick entrance onto a macadam road in general disrepair with cracks and potholes, Niels sat next to Nina in the back of Enrico's car, taking in the sight before him. On both sides of the road were weedy, untended fields lined with unruly vines on rotting stakes. Farther up were rows of scraggly fruit trees that were as naked as skeletons.

"Was this place a vineyard at one time?" Niels asked.

"Yes," Nina said, "my grandmother came here when it was still functioning." She waved her hand toward the ravaged fields and told Niels that this was a grand place in the 1920s. Then when the Civil War came, Aristo's family abandoned the property, and no one returned until the late forties. "There is a mural of it in the foyer when it was in its prime." Nina shrugged as if to say, "That's the way it is." "Now Aristo cares little about maintaining the land. Only his art."

"I hope he has room for me tonight."

"Of course," Nina said in a casual tone.

"I have no choice. Someone canceled my room for today."

"How fortunate," Nina said through a keen, little smile. "Now you will experience Bar … ceee … looo … naaa." She slipped her arm inside his. "Paco, you will not regret this evening."

They parked in a circular gravel drive with an array of cars anywhere from the condition of the Enrico's Audi to a long, black Bentley limousine with a uniformed chauffeur standing next to it. Niels wondered if this wasn't supposed to be Nina's ride from the airport before a late change of plans. She seemed the type of woman comfortable with any class of people.

The old mansion was a semi-decrepit adobe structure with a russet tiled roof with a bell tower. Ivy grew uncontrollably up the splotchy white walls into the eaves and all the way to the base of the bell tower's stone facade, which was covered in green moss. Tangles of rosebushes in need of pruning lined one side of the building in weedy beds.

Outside Niels did a quick survey of his two companions. Nina could have passed for a fashion model, dressed in spiked high heels, designer jeans, and a mauve silk blouse. Enrico had cleaned himself up somewhat, his hair washed and combed and his face shaved. He wore cutoff jeans and a tank top that revealed a tattoo on his arm of a skeleton pirate wearing an eye patch and holding crossed swords. How perfect.

They made their way up the stone walk, which appeared recently cleaned with a few remnants of a mossy patina still clinging like little green eyesores.

Niels thought them an odd threesome as he walked between the short Spaniard on one side and the statuesque and unfathomable Nina on the other.

Waiting at the timber-framed front door with an arched amber transom was a man in his late fifties dressed in a denim work shirt. "Nina," he said, raising his hand in greeting. He had the look of a peasant with a ruddy-colored face, sturdy body, and massive hands with thick, labor-worn fingers that looked capable of bending a sixteen-penny nail.

Nina smiled a hello and spoke in a language that sounded similar to Spanish but faster with a more musical intonation.

The man bowed his head to Nina, nodded sideways to Enrico, and then turned his gaze on Niels. His eyes were deep-set and dark with an old world look as if they belonged to another century. "Señor bienvenida." He then ambled off.

"Were you speaking Greek, Nina?" Niels inquired.

She waved her hand dismissively. "Oh, I lived in Greece with a fellow artist," she said as she watched the Greek remove an overnight bag from the trunk of Enrico's car. "I love language almost as much as art." She grabbed Niels's arm and directed him toward the door. "I speak also Italian, French, and enough German to get me into trouble." She looked at Niels, and a smile creased the corner of her mouth. It seemed like it was meant only for him. It was a reckless little smile as if she was remembering some German escapade.

As if on cue, Enrico clutched the cast-iron door handle and swung open the heavy door. Niels entered the foyer with Nina latched onto his arm. "Paco, it is nice to be with a big, tall man." She raised her foot and turned the long heel of her black pump toward Niels. "I am free to dress tall tonight."

Enrico glanced at Niels and then Nina, a gleam in his eyes. "You told me you like short men."

"Oh, Enrico, mi amor," she said. "I like all men."

The air inside was cool like a cavern. Off to the left was a hand-carved staircase with ornate balusters and banisters with newels missing. The treads appeared sturdy, but the entire structure appeared in need of general repair and refinishing. The foyer floor was made of ocher-hued flagstones with the mortared seams in need of pointing. The walls were constructed of heavy stones, and the ceiling was arched and supported by massive oak beams.

On one wall was the mural of the estate with the mansion in pristine condition. The abode walls were a sparkling white and in stunning contrast to beds of radiant rosebushes clinging to trellises neatly spaced along both sides. The bountiful land teemed with trees bearing apples and pears, and the vineyard was flush with grapevines. There was a gaiety to it, with a bright sky that showered light onto the land. It was a beautiful work from another time and place.

"You like it, aye, Paco," Nina said.

"Yes, very much."

"My grandmother painted it."

Niels turned to Nina. "Really?"

She extended her hand in the direction of three stone steps at the end of the foyer. "Come, Paco," she said merrily as the three of them walked past a library to their right with beautiful inlay cabinetry stuffed with a collection of thick leather-bound books. Even from a distance, there was a dusky, neglected look with furniture draped in drop cloth.

Atop the steps was a massive room with nary a stick of furniture. A fieldstone fireplace anchored the far wall. Cathedral-style windows overlooked the property along one side, and arched openings on the other led to a dining area with a long oak table and high-backed chairs.

"Where is everyone?" Niels said.

"Come," Nina said, "this way."

At the far end of the room, French doors opened onto a veranda, an open-air expanse with a view of the vineyard and a line of jagged mountains. There was a hodgepodge of people talking and mingling. Some were dressed expensively—women in high heels and evening gowns and men in expensive suits—others in slacks and shirts, and a few groups of young people wearing tee shirts and shorts.

A wrought iron railing that was peeling black paint snaked around the kidney-shaped perimeter in stark contrast to the pale-blue marble floor flecked with bits of shiny mica. A bar was set up in a corner with two bartenders wearing crisp white shirts, black vests, and red bow ties. Two waiters in similar attire scooted about serving people.

Nina steered Niels and Enrico toward the railing at the far end. En route she was stopped three times by guests who hugged and kissed her on both of her cheeks.

"Paco, what would you like to drink?"

"Tonic water, please."

Nina lowered her brow, squinting as if making sure she had heard correctly. "Tonic water?"

"I do not imbibe," Niels said. "Tonic water, please."

A wickedly sly grin formed in the corner of Nina's mouth. "Very well." She waved her hand to a waiter. "Camarero, pronto."

The man zipped over. "Sí, Señorita Nina."

She spoke in rapid-fire Spanish. "I told him to put grenadine and a lime peel in your drink. It will add some life to your evening, Paco."

When their drinks arrived, Enrico removed them from the tray one at a time. He handed Nina a red wine and Niels his drink, and he took a glass of beer for himself.

"Salute." Enrico raised his glass as did Nina, who turned to Niels. "Paco?"

"Oh, sorry," he said as he clinked the glasses.

"I leave you two tall people alone," Enrico said as he waved to a lively group wearing sandals or sneakers and a couple of the women who were barefoot. There was an invigorating energy coming from these chattering bohemian types who talked and laughed as if in a communal conversation. And when Enrico arrived, he was greeted with hoots and shouts of affection. "Enrico! Amigo! Dar la bienvenida." There was much kissing of cheeks.

Nina led Niels around and introduced him to some guests, most of whom spoke excellent English, and Aristo, who was a thin, angular man of fifty with gray hair pulled back in a ponytail. "So nice to meet you, Pac … ooo." He pronounced Niels's new moniker with an exaggerated twist. He studied the big American in much the same fashion as Enrico had, sizing up this rare species. "If there is anything I can get you, please do not hesitate to ask." Aristo tilted his head down and off to the side as if he was granting a wish to a subject.

Something about this character put Niels on edge. Could he, along with Enrico, pull some outlandish prank on the Americano with Nina's blessing? He must stay vigilant this evening. "Thank you," Niels said, "that is very kind of you."

Aristo eyed Niels's empty drink and reached for it. "Let me refresh your drink."

"Tonic water, please."

"Oooh," Aristo purred, "you are *abstemio*?" He turned to Nina, and they exchanged looks as if they were members of a secret club. Niels would use his birding instincts to watch and observe. He would stay quiet and look for any sudden movement.

Nina reached her arm around Niels's waist, tightened her grip, and leaned her breast into his side. How wildly marvelous she felt. "Aristo and I are old friends."

"Oh?"

Nina leaned away from Niels for a moment and said hello to a barefoot woman of no more than twenty in jeans and a low-cut halter top, her ample breasts nearly exposed. She reminded Niels of a flower child from the sixties.

Nina said, "Aristo was the artist I spent three years living with in Tuscany, painting the beautiful land."

"Is he Italian?"

"Oh, no." Nina laughed. "Though half Spanish, he is all Greek."

Niels wasn't sure what exactly she meant. Something sexual he assumed, as he took in the eclectic gathering. Nina and her friends were a strange and fascinating group that seemed to have a different way of living—people who, Niels imagined, didn't abide by the morals and rules of his world of routine. It was a predictable cycle that he had existed in like a trained bear.

It would not surprise him if an orgy broke out at some point this evening. And if it did, he decided, he would take it all in like an anthropologist observing the mating rituals of a unique tribe—Euro artists. The idea of engaging in such a thing was incomprehensible and beyond anything he had ever considered.

The closest he could possibly relate to it were a few occasions on business trips when women at company socials had attempted to break Niels's fidelity. The first time he was sitting by himself, tonic water in hand, when a woman who had had too much to drink ground her hips into his shoulder. She had leaned over and whispered in his ear her hotel room number and told him in no uncertain terms what she planned to do with him in private. He had sat there frozen, the smell of whiskey sours, tobacco, and perfume still enveloping him, unable to move or think until the woman straightened herself and staggered away.

Over the years Niels became vigilant in nipping these occurrences before they happened. Usually there was flirting on a woman's part, and he would immediately excuse himself and find cover. He would usually join a group discussion, but later he found it easier to leave.

There had been little contact with girls while he was attending prep school. The summer after graduation, when he metamorphosed from roly-poly nerd into tall and handsome man, Niels stocked shelves at a grocery store back home, his third tour of duty. But this time things were different, as he garnered an abundance of requests from women as to where to find something. "Oh, silly me," one middle-aged woman said with an appraising look at this young Adonis. "Are you new here?" she said, still giving him the once-over. Niels got that more than a few times, as it seemed his old self had been invisible to these women who had never shown any interest the previous summers of his employment.

And then he was off to a small private college in upstate New York—student loan and partial scholarship—where his newfound popularity among women began in earnest. He found it befuddling and more than a bit unsettling—a phone call in the middle of the night, a slurred female voice at the other end inviting him to come over to her dorm room, or a coed waiting for him to depart a class and walking alongside him, talking him up in an aggressive manner. At least he took it that way. Others might have called it friendly. Shy to the core, he retreated to his studies and birding.

Then he met Laura, a pretty girl with the smile of a beauty queen. Her eyes had nary a trace of ogling admiration but a look that he mistook as righteous and lovely. She was a confident, God-fearing girl who was a member of the youth ministry that she convinced Niels to join.

Soon he was dating his first and only girlfriend, and Laura let it be known on campus that *pretty boy* was spoken for. Both were virgins, and Laura made sure it stayed that way, not that Niels was overly aggressive during their timid make-out sessions in a movie theater or on a park bench. One time—and only one time—he made a move for her breasts and was met by a firm grip on his wrist and a sharp, "No."

But dating Laura opened a whole new world. He had someone who was not only a girlfriend but a person with strong opinions on current events and campus politics. And in that bloom of romance, he thought he had found the right girl to spend the rest of his life with.

A few years into the marriage, Niels's developed a stigmatism that required thick-lens glasses. And then when he grew heavy, women left him alone except on those occasions when they seemed to see through the fleshy cheeks and beyond the thick eyeglasses and captured a glimpse of the handsome young man he used to be.

Now, here in Spain, he wondered how Nina saw him.

Chapter 4

Aristo returned pronto with Niels's drink, this time in a tall glass with a straw. "Your drink," he said, "tonic water and grenadine with a twist."

"Thank you."

"My pleasure," Aristo said before he turned to mingle among his guests.

The grenadine did add a sweet flavor that toned down the bitterness of the tonic water. Niels considered that it might be spiked, but he convinced himself that it had none of the strong smell or harsh taste of alcohol.

Nina gestured to the view off the railing. "Montserrat Mountain is lovely, no?"

It was spectacular with the rosy peaks backdropped by a rich blue sky. "I thought that was a series of mountains," Niels said.

"No," Nina said, "one mountain with a series of peaks." A look of serious modesty came over her face. "In the mountain is a retreat for Benedictine monks with a holy grotto where the Virgin Mary is purported to have visited." There was a question in her tone but also respect.

"Do you believe in heavenly visitation?"

Nina shrugged away the question. "The church bells, oh," she said, raising her hand as if to say, "This is the truth." "Those bells echoing against the great mountain of stone is a lovely thing. Like art for the ears." She looked at Niels, her eyes glinting with passion. "That is what I believe."

For a moment silence fell between them. Out of habit, Niels looked over the property for birds but saw none. There was an old stable and barn in need of paint and repair in front of a pasture enclosed by corral fencing. There wasn't any livestock in sight, and the land and the buildings seemed deserted as far the eye could see. The temperature was warm. But there was little humidity, and Niels felt a pleasantness overcome him as he continued to sip the sweet cherry-colored concoction.

A waiter came by with a tray of hors d'oeuvres of prosciutto and goat cheese on wafer-thin crackers. Niels was suddenly famished and took a few more and washed them down with his drink. "Oh, those appetizers are wonderful," he said as general conversation.

Nina smiled her secret smile and took Niels's empty glass and handed it to the waiter. Again a rapid-fire order. In no time the server returned, handing Niels his drink. In the other he offered the tray. "Aperitivo, señor?"

"Thank you," Niels said as he plopped another savory hors d'oeuvre in his mouth. Oh, how very tasty. Niels vigilance in observing for any subterfuge was fading, seemingly unimportant at the moment, as he was flushed with a sense of well-being. How good and grand it was to be here, carefree as the breeze that blew gently across the veranda, bringing with it the faint scent of roses.

A gentleman impeccably dressed in a tan suit with a carnation in the lapel came up to Nina and spoke to her in Spanish.

"Paco," Nina said, "I would like to introduce you to Count Federico de Maya."

With the handsome dark features of a well-aging matinee idol, the Count stood an inch or so shorter than Niels. His hair was tinged gray on the side, and his face had the ruddy, healthy complexion of an outdoorsman. His eyes flickered with an air of the devil about him, as if he could get down and dirty if need be. They shook hands.

"My apologies for my limousine not retrieving you from Barcelona airport." The Count tilted his head forward in a mini bow.

Nina said, "Federico is a birdwatcher like you, Paco."

"How interesting," Niels said as the beverages and food seemed to have transported him to a state of Nirvana. His entire body was relaxed and at ease. He felt wonderful, so utterly wonderful. "Say, Count, what can you tell me about Ebro Delta?"

"There is nothing like it," Federico said with proprietary pride. "Mountains, plains, wetland, and the birds—oh, those beautiful birds." He extended his hand, and with a relaxed and delicate movement, he tapped Niels wrist. "Citril finch, pin-tailed sandgrouse, glossy ibis, purple heron—" He took a short breath as if to regain his bearing. "You must excuse me. I do love birding so."

To Niels's surprise, he had finished his drink and raised his glass over his head. "Nina, uno mas, pronto."

Nina clicked her fingers and caught the waiter's eye, who made a beeline for the bar.

"Count," Niels said in a voice so loud that he startled himself. He brought his hand to his mouth and said in a husky whisper, "I plan to bird-watch at Ebro Delta."

The waiter handed the big American his drink, and Niels hooted in a drawn-out voice, "Thank yoouuu." He threw away the straw and took a deep swallow. "Ah," he growled, "that's what I'm talking about." Niels had no idea where his words came from, but what the heck! It was fun to act a bit out of character as he looked around to see if anyone had noticed him. To his pleasant surprise, a few groups were laughing and dancing to Flamenco music coming from two wall speakers. There was an energetic staccato style to the exaggerated movements of the dancers that seemed more humorous than serious.

That new little motor humming away inside Niels fed off the dancers. "Nina," Niels shouted, "I have a dance I would like to show you." He threw down the remainder of his drink in one hearty gulp and tossed his empty glass behind his shoulder and off the balcony.

"Yes, Paco," Nina said as she opened her palms toward him. "Dance for me."

Niels began flapping his arms in the air, chirping out, "Beezeep, beezeep," as he circled around Nina. She began laughing in great bursts as Niels continued around her like Big Bird gone wild. "Federico," Niels called as he continued his routine around Nina.

"Yes, Paco," the Count said in a bemused tone.

"This is my version of the mating dance of the American woodcock."

By this time Nina was laughing so hard that tears were streaming down her cheeks as Niels continued to flap and gyrate around her.

When the song ended, Niels bowed to Nina with arms extended out to his side. He turned to Federico and stuck out his chest and extended his arms, raising and lowering them like a bird ready to take flight. "There is nothing in the world better than birding."

"Almost nothing," Federico said through a thin, knowing smile.

Chapter 5

Niels stirred from the sound of a catlike purr in his ear. He could not remember such a deep sleep. He tried to awaken but felt trapped as if stuck in that sleepy limbo between the conscious and unconscious mind.

In his dreamlike state, he felt the weight of a body on top of him, a soft yet sinewy female body rubbing against his chest.

The coarse, toad-like lashes of a tongue inside his ear canal awoke him. Shafts of morning light caused him to blink as he saw the blurry image of a long and lean woman's body lying on top of him. *Oh my God,* he thought as bits and pieces of last night cascaded in his mind. There was much laughter, and Niels had a foggy memory of singing and dancing with a circle of people around him as everyone gyrated to the beat of the Flamenco music. He had felt oh so grand.

"Paco, you awake," Nina whispered in his ear.

"My glasses," Niels said, "have you seen my glasses?"

"Let's not worry about that right now," Nina said as she ran her hand down his torso and took hold of his private parts. "You look much better without them."

A wild romp last night in this very large bed with Nina warbled in his mind. He felt obligated to remove himself from her viper-like grasp, but his newly awakened carnal side overwhelmed him as Nina straightened up, legs straddling, and brought him inside her. Good Lord, this woman had a way about her as she rocked back and forth.

This was all so very different to Niels, who had never ventured beyond the missionary position with his lifetime partner and wife, Laura. Sex to them had been a composed affair of once a week.

They had both taken pleasure from it, or at least Niels thought Laura had. They never discussed it, but every Saturday morning after coffee and the newspaper, they went upstairs and undressed. Without any foreplay, they would have sex.

"I ride you," Nina said with a pronounced rolling of the "R." "Like the wild stallion that you are, Paco."

Niels thrusted upward and lifted Nina much like a child riding a dime-store pony.

When he and Laura were first married, one problem was her difficulty with Niels's well-endowed organ, especially the girth. Eventually she seemed to adapt, but there were instances when she would wince if he got carried away. So he always tried to maintain his composure, never pushing too hard.

"Oh, Paco," Nina moaned as he unleashed his third deposit. Where it all was coming from, he had not a clue. Nina rolled off Niels and rested her head on his shoulder. "You had good time last night, big boy," she said, wiggling his semi-flaccid member. "Yes?"

"Yes, I did," Niels said. "Do you know where my glasses are?"

Nina nuzzled Niels's neck and said, "You broke them dancing, you wild man."

"You spiked my drink last night," Niels said in an even voice. He rolled on his side to face Nina, but she was only a blur.

"You are not mad," Nina said, "are you, Paco?"

"I certainly should be," Niels said as he reached over and brought her into his arms, "but I will allow you to make it up to me."

Chapter 6

Niels found his shirt and trousers at the foot of the bed, but his underwear and socks were nowhere to be found. He felt helpless without his glasses. Another pair was in his luggage at the hotel. He took stock of himself and was rather amazed that he didn't have a hangover of any sort. As a matter of fact, he felt invigorated. And when Nina returned with coffee, he'd be even better, he told himself, in spite of the fact that the John Muir in him was nagging him about his lack of moral judgment.

He had been right in suspecting Nina and her cohorts of subterfuge. He had had a general idea of what was going on in the middle of his second drink and could have stopped. But that new little motor humming away inside him had fed off Nina and her wildly animated world accompanied by its cast of characters as last night came into focus. He had been the biggest character, prancing about barefoot in his skivvies, bopping and stomping to the beat of a late-arriving Mariachi band. At some point in his inebriated state, he knew for certain he would never again be the straight arrow he had always been.

And now in his sober state, he confirmed it. There was no going back. Who he would become, he wasn't sure, but the fact of the matter was that he felt like a new man, a different man here in Spain, thousands of miles away from his home and his regulated orbit.

Nina returned without coffee and told him that Enrico had already departed. "I have called a taxi to get us back."

"You didn't see my shoes about, did you?"

"There is a pile of shoes downstairs, Paco."

"Oh, yes," Niels said through a thin smile, "quite a time last night."

"The Count was very impressed with your mating dance." Nina ran her hand over Niels's short-trimmed hair and laughed. "The wild birdman came out in you last night."

After he found his shoes on the veranda, Niels also found the remains of his bent and crushed glasses. He stuffed them in his pocket and went outside with Nina to wait for the taxi. He never did find his underwear.

On the ride back to the hotel, Nina asked Niels if he wanted to bird-watch with the Count.

"I would love to bird with him."

Nina punched a number on her cell phone and had a conversation in Spanish. She was laughing and chuckling, wagging her finger at Niels as if he were someone who amused her greatly.

Nina hung up. "Federico ask one favor of you."

Niels looked at her, and she stared back, her lip trembling before she broke out in a great guffaw.

Niels had an idea where this was going but walked into it anyway. "Yes, Nina, what is it?"

"That you keep your clothes on at Ebro Delta."

Niels shook his head and looked down for a moment. "Was I that bad?"

"Far from it. Federico said he always wondered about the mating dance of your American woodcock, and now he has seen it firsthand." Nina slapped Niels on the thigh. "He had a splendid time with you last night. He said that besides himself, you are the craziest birder he has ever met."

"When did you schedule me?" Niels saw the irony that another woman was planning his life.

"Day after tomorrow, Paco. Federico will take you in his chauffeured car, no less."

"Was that the one parked in front of Aristo's?"

"Yes," Nina said as she leaned forward and gave instructions to the driver and then turned back to Niels. "His family is very wealthy." She smiled and said, "As they say in your country, he comes from old money."

"Thank you," Niels said. "One more favor, if I might."

"Yes, anything."

"Would you come into the hotel with me? I really can't see well enough to get myself around in there."

"Of course," Nina said as she tapped Niels's arm. "For you, anything."

Nina took care of securing Niels's luggage and talked the clerk into giving him an upgraded room because of the arrival date snafu that Niels was certain she had caused. This woman seemed to have no limit to getting people to do what she wanted.

When the luggage was brought around front, they followed the porter up to the room. Niels handed Nina his wallet. "Please pay him, Nina. I can't make out the currency."

"Certainly, Paco," she said as she removed a bill and thanked the man. She then handed Niels back his wallet.

"It seems nice," Niels said rather hesitantly as he looked over his living quarters. He could make out blurry images of an open sitting area with a table and chairs, a king-size bed, and a spacious bathroom. He then lifted his suitcase, computer bag, and his carry-on up onto the bed.

"You tell me where to look, Paco, and I will be your eyes."

"There should be a zippered compartment on the side of the suitcase." Niels heard the sound of the zipper opening. "Nothing there," she said, stepping back from the bed.

"That can't be." Niels reached for the compartment and found it empty and realized that Laura had always packed his extra pair.

Nina removed every article of clothing—slacks and shirts, slippers, low-cut hiking shoes for birding, underwear, etc. "I don't see them in here," Nina said. "Maybe the other bags."

After they emptied everything, Niels glasses were nowhere to be found. "Oh my God," he said, "I don't think I packed them. I am lost without my glasses." Niels felt a pang of appreciation for Laura's management of his life.

"Do not worry." Nina got on her cell phone and began speaking in Spanish in a friendly, soothing manner of one asking an old friend for a big favor. She hung up and said, "We have an appointment with an optometrist, Dr. Carlos Santiago, in one hour."

"What?" Niels heard the incredulity in his voice. "How did you arrange this?"

"Hah, you must have faith in Nina. Carlos is my cousin, and he owes me big time, as they say in your country."

"You're something else, Nina," Niels said. "Something else."

Dr. Santiago's office was a short cab ride from the hotel, and they made it there right on time. Niels had read that nothing in Spain ever went on schedule, and he was surprised when he and Nina were whisked into an examination room. The cloudy figure of what Niels assumed was the doctor entered. He and Nina exchanged a warm embrace and greetings. "Carlos," Nina said, "this is my friend, Paco."

Niels extended his hand and felt the firm grip of a soft yet strong hand. "Thank you, Doctor. Niels Pettigrew here."

"Of course, Mr. Pettigrew. Any friend of Nina's is a friend of mine. Now let me examine your eyes, and then I will give you an eye test." The doctor's voice had the same upper-class resonance as Federico's.

After all the testing was completed, the doctor began to speak, and Nina interrupted, "Carlos, what about a pair of contact lenses."

Niels said, "Yes, that's a good idea. Contact lens would be great … and an extra pair of glasses too."

"Stylish glasses," Nina said as she went to the carousel and removed a pair and handed them to Niels. He ran his hand over the thin frame and looped his finger inside the smaller lens opening than his old glasses. "They feel good," Niels said. "Okay, these will work."

"Very good," Carlos said, "I can get you a pair of contacts by late today, but the glasses may not be until tomorrow."

"Really?" Niels said. "I thought it would be the other way around."

"I have a friend who can make this happen," Carlos said nonchalantly.

Outside Carlos's office, the blare and hum of traffic seemed more intense as his suddenly acute hearing could distinguish the nuances of the sounds.

Nina suggested lunch at an outdoor café on a pedestrian side street.

Niels squinted at the scene before him, the indistinguishable people passing by. The buildings looked like gray mounds. His weakened eyesight had added distance from his old self as if another part of whom he used to be had been stripped from his DNA. "Lunch sounds like a grand idea."

Nina took hold of his arm and began to lead him down the street. "I will be your eyes."

A part of Niels still had second thoughts about what he had gotten himself into. Was he just some toy she could play with for a while and then dispense with? But he would do nothing to discourage his attraction to her. Nina had kick-started his life, and to think of turning away from her, even with all her wiles, did not seem an option.

Nina jerked Niels arm as she suddenly turned a corner. "This way, Paco. The café is not far."

In midstep, Niels shifted himself to his right, nearly toppling over into Nina.

"You are like a big vessel lost at sea." Nina laughed as she regained her balance.

"And you are my tugboat guiding me home."

"Hah." Nina latched onto Niels's arm and steered him down the street.

Lunch was one big blur—the food, the waiter, even Nina. But her voice, that ever-modulating vocal instrument, kept Niels at ease. One moment it was the sexy seductress, and next it was the bawdy laughter, the confidential friend, and so many others that Niels lost himself in listening to her. She would have made a great actress, or maybe, he thought in a moment of reflection, she was acting with him.

After Niels handed Nina his wallet and she paid the bill with euros that Laura had ordered a month before at their bank, he said, "What do you say you give me a tour of the cathedral near my hotel?"

A big smile split Nina's face, a smile that even a blind man could see, a bright radiant smile that could bring any ship lost at sea home safely. "Yes, Paco, I will guide you to the Cathedral of the Holy Cross and Saint Eulalia." There was a tremor of respect and awe in her voice as if this was a great duty for her to undertake.

Outside the cathedral, Nina described in detail the roof with a variety of gargoyles. She told the history of the structure, "Built from the thirteenth through the fifteenth century, but most of it was done in the fourteenth." She raised her hands toward the building. "But the neo-Gothic facade was constructed in the nineteenth century, which was common to Catalan churches." Her voice was an even keel, no dramatics here, just the facts but with a trace of Spanish pride for what her ancestors had accomplished.

Inside, she described the intricacies of the vaulted ceiling over five aisles. She painted a picture with her words, the artist using all her skills to present what Niels eyes could not see. But in his mind he saw it all so very clearly, and at the same time, he gained respect for Nina. Her knowledge of the cathedral would have made any tour guide proud. But beyond that was the fact that this woman was intelligent and thoughtful with a deep appreciation for this magnificent piece of art. And this was a different side to her, the artist in an artistic setting, different from the free spirit hanging out at an old run-down mansion with other artists. Here she was standing in the midst of something magnificent and beautiful, and her demeanor was that of respect.

* * *

Back in the examination room, Carlos fitted the lens into Niels's eyes, and finally he could see. He took a good look at Dr. Carlos Santiago—medium height, thinning gray-black hair, and candid green eyes that gave the impression he was a hell-raiser in his youth.

"How is your vision, Mr. Pettigrew?" the doctor asked.

"Wonderful, just wonderful," Niels said. "It is good to have my vision back."

"Nothing blurry or uncomfortable?" the doctor asked.

Niels shrugged. "Nothing."

"You look so handsome, Paco," Nina said, purring. "Doesn't he, Carlos?"

Carlos smiled at his cousin with a look of familiarity. It was a deep probing look of one who understood this woman better than most. "Yes," Carlos said with a laugh, "your Paco is *un hombre guapo.*" The doctor handed Niels a hand mirror.

Niels was surprised by what he saw. Yes, there was some excess in the cheeks, and the neck was a bit fleshy. But there was a handsomeness that he hadn't seen since he had been a young man. It was more than the thick glasses, as it seemed his outlook had added confidence to his appearance that resulted in a firmer jawline, and his eyes had a sparkle of one on a great adventure. "Not bad. Not bad at all," Niels said.

Carlos then said, "We also have a surprise." He handed Niels two cases, and inside each was a pair of tortoiseshell glasses.

Niels studied them for a moment and then looked at Carlos and then Nina. "I must say, Nina, I do like them. Thank you."

"Try one on, Paco."

He put on a pair and looked back in the mirror. They gave him a professorial look but without a trace of nerdiness. "It's amazing," Niels said as he nodded his approval. "Whatever was I thinking wearing my old pair." He returned them to the case. "These will be great." He smiled and turned to Nina. "I look and feel like a new man."

"You are, Paco. You are," Nina said in a merry tone.

Carlos told Niels that he had to ease his way into wearing the contacts. "Two hours at a time the first day. Four the next—"

Niels nodded and said, "How about you join Nina and me for drinks and dinner tonight?" Part of him was amazed at the words coming out of his mouth, but the other was in control—firm control.

"Grand idea, Paco," Nina said, her eyes shining like dark spheres radiating with a look that said, "I like you and your spirit." But he couldn't help but wonder how long that glimmer in Nina's eyes would remain. "I like all men," she had told Enrico in Niels's presence. How many others like Niels had she transformed and then tired of.

It was arranged that Nina and Carlos would meet Niels at his hotel at nine that evening. Niels told them to meet him at the bar, figuring they would be late. In the meantime he decided to do some sightseeing in Barcelona.

At El Hotel Catalán, which was situated in the middle of a historic district called Barri Gotic, Niels asked a few questions to the concierge over a local map and headed out.

Five minutes from the hotel, Niels came upon a lovely outdoor café on a raised stone patio under a maple tree. People sat at small tables, chatting amicably over coffee and croissants. A three-story building made of gray fieldstones presented a perfect backdrop, with arch entryways and wrought iron and latticed work touches.

Niels ambled about, taking in one charming, traffic-free street after another with shops, tapas bars, and cafés. He took in Carrer de Pi church, a fifteen-century stone structure where he enjoyed a free choral performance. What struck him while he was walking was the more relaxed pace of the people, so different from Philadelphia. He remembered an old saying. Americans lived to work, and Europeans worked to live.

For years, absorbed in his work, Niels fit that description to a T. And his wife took control of the remainder of his life, but with one exception—birding. The first year of marriage, Laura arranged for her and Niels to help out at a homeless shelter the same weekend of the annual bird fest at Hawk Mountain to watch the bald eagles migrate to Florida.

"I'm birding," Niels had said with some grit in his tone, a tone Laura had never heard before. Ever since, she stayed on top of the bird-watching events, and conflicts never again arose.

At the time, it seemed easier having an efficient wife to allow him to devote his energies to business. Now it seemed here in Spain, Nina was making those decisions for him but in a new and exciting direction, all because an airplane was in the wrong place at the wrong time. Niels had looked up wind shear. The definition read, "A microscale meteorological phenomenon occurring over a very small distance." The actuary in him considered the odds of an airplane running into wind shear—a very rare occurrence, indeed.

As a result of that rare occurrence, he was here in Europe without his wife, a bachelor, and he was transformed into someone at the fiesta she would not have known, someone who would have appalled her. Throughout his life Niels had led an orderly existence without glitches or the arrival of unexpected events. Now he was in a world where he was going with the flow as if a free spirit had wrested his soul from his old self. It came over him that his relationship to Laura had evolved away from what he had interpreted as love when they first met to dependency by the time she died.

Out of the tragic death of a woman from which he feared he might never recover, he found himself in Barcelona with a whole new world to experience ahead of him.

On the way back to the hotel, Niels decided to stop in a tapas bar and—dare he think it—have a drink. Nina had told him that he had drunk vodka at Aristo's fiesta, but he felt like something new.

The place had a humming energy to it. There were heavy hunks of ham legs lathered in fat dangling from the ceiling and a display case with a colorful array of olives and cheese, seafood, bread, and a variety of meats. Color was everywhere, from the amber wood paneling to the lime green chalkboard behind the bar with the listed specials. Niels spotted an empty stool and took a seat. It dawned on him this was the first time in his life he had ever sat at a bar. This trip, he thought, would have many firsts. Niels had a basic grasp of Spanish, but he could understand little of the mach speed the people were speaking. After a couple of minutes of being ignored, Niels raised his hand and said in an assertive voice, "Por favor, por favor."

The bartender looked up from pouring beer from the tap. "Sí, señor."

"Cerveza," Niels said. Beer was the only alcoholic beverage he knew the name for, and he didn't feel like speaking English. Something about it would have ruined the Spanish experience.

The bartender raised a tall glass with dark-red beer that he had poured.

"Bueno," Niels said.

The bartender placed the beer on the counter, an inquiring glint in his eyes. Niels sensed he knew he was an American. "Ración?" the man said.

"Que?"

The bartender smiled and said, "Tapas."

"Sí." Niels was enjoying himself exchanging words in a foreign tongue.

The bartender went down to the display case and returned with a platter of pita bread, olives and cheese, salsa, and a skewer of meat.

Walking had made Niels hungry, and he placed a piece of meat on a pita and added some salsa. It was delicious. He grabbed the beer and noted it was room temperature. It had a bite to it and brought to mind a strong, bitter root beer. This red beverage would do just fine.

As Niels sat drinking his beer and finishing off his tapas, he listened to the voices of passionate people. It seemed there were a variety of discussions. Some talked about soccer—complete with a kicking demonstration. He heard others talk of literature. Miguel de Cervantes's name was bandied about, and a young couple next to Niels who spoke in reverent tones talked about art and even mentioned Picasso. "Pi … cass … soo."

Niels imagined Nina interjecting her two cents and more into the conversation with a special twist of Spanish bravado in her voice like a matador waving a red flag at El Toro.

He wondered if her grandmother had really had an affair with the great artist. If she was anything like Nina, he would not put it past her. Never in his life had he met anyone like the sultry Nina, who took on life as if each day could be her last, a woman the complete opposite of his wife of twenty-five years. Laura would have found Nina's conduct—from her suggestive language to her uninhibited delight in sex—the sign of a person with low morals. Laura went so far as to not read books with even a hint of explicit sex or go to similar movies. "What is the world coming to with sex infiltrating every part of our society?" she often said. He pondered the thought that Laura had been a stilting influence on his life.

He told himself he wished she were with him. Not in this bar, of course, he thought as he finished his tapas and took his time with his beer, which had mellowed him out. He was at peace and so very relaxed, but he knew he needed to be careful with his intake, for his threshold for intoxication must surely be low. Niels was tempted to have another but instead paid and left for his hotel.

Back in his room, he stretched out atop the bed with his biography of John Muir.

After ten pages, Niels was having trouble keeping his eyes open. Walking in the late afternoon heat and the beer had made him pleasantly sleepy. He checked the clock on the nightstand—7:00 p.m.—and set the alarm for 8:30 p.m.

Niels woke to the beat of salsa music mixed with static crackling. A dream flashed in his mind. In it John Muir and Laura had arrived at Aristo's fiesta. The great man was barefoot and wearing a drab brown outdoorsman jacket with baggy pockets. His long beard gave him a bohemian look that fit right in with the eccentric artist types. Laura wore a dress to her ankles with long sleeves and a bonnet on her head.

They both warned Niels of the evils of alcohol and said that his shameful, drunken behavior had shocked them. Muir jabbed his finger in a scolding manner at Niels. "That woman," he said as he stared at Nina, his eyes furrowed slits, "will be the damnation of your soul." Laura pursed her lips, shaking her head in disgust. "Whatever are you thinking consorting with *these* people, Niels?"

Nina stood naked, her pubic hairs abundant and curled black, laughing at both of them. "Oh, John, Laura," she said in a light, airy tone as she reached for John's hand, "come and dance with us." John Muir had a look of utter consternation as he jerked away from Nina's grasp and grabbed Laura by the elbow.

They faded away into the air. Nina laughed and said, "Oh, Paco, your friends were—" She paused for a moment, searching for the right words. "Old fuddy-duddies."

Niels put on his new glasses and looked at the cover of the book with John Muir standing at the edge of a creek, wilderness all around, dressed in the same clothes as in his dream. Niels agreed with Nina in his dream. He did look like an old fuddy-duddy. For a moment he thought of Laura in the pilgrim dress before he dismissed the thought from his mind; he got out of bed and put the book in the bottom of his suitcase and piled clothes on top.

At nine o'clock Niels entered the half-filled hotel bar, wearing his contacts. It had a sleek modern appearance with a faux steel trim and bright colors. It was the type of place Niels used to abhor, but now it seemed palatable. The room had a shiny, metallic bar with six stools, a lounge with comfortable chairs around low glass tables with an outer ring of mosaic tile. Past the lounge was a flagstone open-air patio backdropped by an ivy-covered wall along the far end. A line of colorful rope lights running along the wall's top edge added a festive air, casting an ambient rainbow of hues over the outdoor space.

He took a corner seat at the bar and raised his finger to the bartender. "Cerveza."

"Qué tipo, señor?"

He heard the low murmur of English being spoken at a nearby table and didn't have any qualms. "*Habla* English?"

The bartender smiled. "But of course. What would you like?"

"Red beer." Niels held an open palm over the other and raised it. "A tall one."

The bartender, who was in his late thirties and had the look of one who had seen it all, frowned for a moment and then said through a thin smile. "Certainly, señor."

Halfway through the beer, his guests arrived. Niels stood and shook hands with Carlos. He and Nina exchanged glances. It seemed as though she had never left his side, and they did not need to greet each other. Even when she wasn't physically in his presence, she was often floating in his mind.

Carlos ordered a round of drinks. There was only one seat open at the bar, so Niels suggested they sit in the lounge.

After they got situated at a table near the patio, a smile came over Nina that said, "You are learning." She pointed to Niels's nearly finished beer and said, "Paco, you like the cerveza *roja*?"

Niels drank the remainder of his drink and raised his eyebrows and grinned. "Sí."

The waiter arrived and served their drinks—beer, bourbon straight up, and red wine for Nina. "This one was my second of the day," Niels said as handed his empty glass to the waiter. "I had one earlier in a tapas bar after I walked around the historic district."

Nina looked at Carlos and then Niels. Her eyes were shining and so mysteriously dark and—dare he think it—sexy. She was dressed in a sleeveless black dress that clung tight, accentuating her curvaceous body. They exchanged another look, and Niels felt an immediate pang of lust. He wanted her but wondered what hoops he would have to go through. He knew her well enough to realize that nothing was a sure thing with this exotic woman, who possessed a very adjustable moral compass that could change on a whim. She wore little makeup, and her jet-black hair was tied in a ponytail as if to say to one and all, "Don't tie me down to any sort of style. I can wear chic clothes and a peasant hairdo. So what?"

Niels felt fantastic, and he had a definite goal for this evening—to get Nina into bed and be sober enough to enjoy it. He sipped his beer carefully as Carlos reminisced about growing up in Spain in the late '70s and early '80s. Niels took his age to be around forty-five. Niels sat back and listened as Carlos did most of the talking while Nina seemed comfortable letting him reminisce about their childhood.

They grew up in well-to-do families with a variety of characters. Carlos spoke of an aunt who would spend nine months a year on a cruise ship. "What about Tio Miguel," Nina said at the end of Carlos's story. She told of an uncle who was a curator at El Prado and was charged with theft of a famous art piece, but who was eventually found innocent.

She had the natural storyteller's ability to keep a listener interested by putting a spin on certain words. "He was a scounnnn … drel," she said through a waggish grin. "No one in the family believed him innocent."

"Yes," Carlos added, "but no one held it against him." Nina and Carlos exchanged looks before they burst into laughter. Niels leaned back in his chair and hooted along with them. This was fun. By golly, it was great fun to be in the company of these two interesting people. It came over Niels that the people in his old life were boring and viewed things with tunnel vision.

Carlos spoke with fondness as he told about horseback riding on a great uncle's ranch in "a magnifico valley in Catalonia." He smiled wryly at his cousin. "You remember when we swam naked in the pond?"

"Of course," Nina said as she wagged her finger at her cousin. "You were a bad boy."

Carlos raised his hands in mock protest. "It was your idea," he said. "I did not want to insult you."

Another round of drinks and appetizers were ordered. The beer so far had had little effect on Niels other than total relaxation. He wondered if his size—he weighed 250 pounds—allowed him some leeway in his consumption of this delightful red beer.

Carlos suggested they go to a restaurant frequented by locals on the outskirts of town. "Sounds like a grand idea," Niels said. "A grand idea, indeed. Don't you think so, Nina?"

"Paco, I think you are getting in the spirit of Barcelona."

So off they went in Carlos's Mercedes-Benz sedan. Nina sat next to Niels in the back. He reached over and took her hand in his. Then he brought it to his heart. "You have made me see another side of life," he whispered. "For that I will always be thankful."

She looked at him, and for a moment, as if a curtain were drawn, he saw a trace of vulnerability before she regained her poise and said, "Hah, you are full of surprises."

Sitting next to Nina was exhilarating and intoxicating. He was a schoolboy on his first date with the prom queen. But he must not give too much of himself away. His shrewdness surprised him, and at the same time, it excited him more. This was a game with Nina, he surmised, and he must keep his wits about him. *So listen and talk, but not too much, and keep a distance as if you're a rare species of bird, the impredecible Americano, whom she finds alluring and irresistible.*

The restaurant was along the Mediterranean coastline, situated back in a cluster of pine trees. It was an elegant yet rustic establishment with a nautical decor. A ship's wheel hung behind the bar. Thickly braided ropes looped across a series of beams in the high ceiling, and one wall had a mural of a Spanish fishing village.

Carlos was greeted by the maître d' with a big embrace followed by an exchange of kisses on the cheeks. Carlos introduced Niels and Nina in English to Javier, who bowed his head to Nina and took her hand and kissed it. "Carlos, where have you been hiding this—" The maître d' fluttered his hands in the air, trying to find the words in English before saying, "Esta bella mujer." Nina's lips parted in a bright, passionate smile as though she had been saving it all her life for just this moment and just this man, Javier. In that instant Niels saw in Javier's gaze a look of one who would risk anything for the beautiful woman before him. Javier then turned to Niels and shook his hand firmly. "Welcome, señor. Welcome."

They were seated at a table with a view above a cove with high cliffs, and the sea seemingly stretched to infinity, shining blue-black in the moonlight.

But the moment seemed too perfect. Never had Niels experienced such a sense of bliss. The little voice that told him he was in a different world with a different kind of people said, *Be careful, Niels. Be very careful.*

He thought of Nina's smile to Javier earlier, exposing a sparkling row of teeth that seemed capable of putting any man under her spell but also possessing a sharp bite capable of shattering many a heart.

What would become of him if she dropped him off at his hotel tonight and never appeared again? He didn't know how to contact her or where she lived other than "the other side of town."

The evening progressed with his engaging and seductive company in the fading, softly lit ambience. And as the light in the room dimmed, so did Nina's mood, which tempered to that of controlled animation. She engaged in conversation, but it was as though her energy had clicked down a notch from seventy-eight revolutions per minute to forty-five. Niels wondered if Carlos had an influence over her, a calming familial presence who understood her completely and in whose company she didn't have to be the center of attention.

The meal was as great as the company. The conversations were light and airy, and Niels had to remember what exactly it was they talked about—a little about art, which he had a passing knowledge of, and soccer, which Carlos was a fanatic about. Nina, it turned out, had once been married for three days to an older artist before she had it annulled, and Carlos was divorced with two children whom he saw on the weekends.

On the ride back, Nina sat in the front. Niels wasn't sure what to make of it. He had expected they would spend the night at his hotel, but nothing had been said. What would he do if she said, "Thank you for dinner, and it was so nice to make your acquaintance," and then drove off, never to be seen again. Then what? *Told you so, Niels,* the voice whispered.

Carlos drove back along the coastline, telling Niels, "It is good for my soul to spend time near the Mediterranean." He mentioned other family incidents, but Nina gave little input. She was unusually quiet.

Niels wanted to say something to her, but the other voice, the one he had discovered in Spain—or more precisely the one Nina had extracted out of a deep, dark place—told him to say little and play it close to the vest. Sitting directly behind her, he placed the back of his hand behind her ponytail and left it on her long, graceful neck, which reminded him of a skittish flamingo he had spotted in the Florida Everglades. At first he had thought it a roseate spoonbill, but as the bird waded closer to the shoreline, Niels realized it was an American flamingo, not common to the Glades.

Nina brought her hand back onto Niels's. He felt the warmth of her touch as a wave of passion seemed to transfer from her hand to his. At that moment he knew she was his.

Carlos pulled his car in front of the hotel, removed an overnight bag from the trunk, and handed it to Niels. Nina remained sitting in the front seat. "Thank you for dinner," Carlos said. "Tonight you are a lucky man." He then opened the front door, and Nina came out. They kissed each other on the cheek. Carlos waved to Niels, and then he was gone.

"Let us have a drink in the bar." Nina came up to Niels, her lovely face in his, her breath warm and inviting. She put her hand behind his neck and leaned into him, kissing his lips. Niels put his arms around her waist and leaned back from her. "A drink sounds great."

The bar was nearly empty. The muted amber light coming from the deserted patio caught their attention. Earlier it had seemed brighter and more alive. Now it had the look of a sunset when the light makes one last stand before it fades into the darkness. As if drawn to it, they went to the patio.

It was one o'clock in the morning, way past Niels's normal bedtime. But he wasn't a bit tired. No, his body was on alert, sexual alert—a new sensation that seemed to have rewired his internal clock. And along with it, his sense of morality had been altered, and to his pleasant surprise, he found it not one bit problematic. Somehow he had transformed from teetotaling birder to the new Niels overnight.

While he was craving sex with Nina in the worse way, he realized he couldn't let her see it. He sensed that the physical act was only part of it with her. The other part, which seemed just as important, was a game. What the rules were and how it was played, Niels wasn't sure. The only thing he was sure of was that he must maintain his poise with her at all times, no matter how uncertain he was internally.

His instincts told him that she hadn't figured him out, hadn't seen all the facets to her new creation, Señor Niels Pettigrew. His new look with the contacts increased her physical attraction to him, and that followed by his immediate agreement to let her guide him blind around the city had surprised her. *Paco, you have spirit.* He also calculated that once she did figure out a man, no matter his spirit, she tired of him. *Hasta la vista.*

There was another couple in a corner of the patio, and they sat at a table along the ivy-covered wall.

A waiter came and lit a candle. Nina's face seemed to radiate with shadowy hues. Never had she looked lovelier. She suggested they share a carafe of cabernet. "Grand idea," Niels said. One more new experience was about to arrive.

The wine had an earthy richness to it.

"You like the wine, Paco?" There was an analytical tone to Nina's voice, far different from the first time he met her on the plane.

"Marvelous," Niels said with raised eyebrows. "I am completely enjoying your corruption of me."

"I have just begun, Paco."

Chapter 7

Nina sat on the end of the Niels's bed. "Paco, you want me?"

He removed his shoes and socks, his shirt, and then his trousers. He stood before her in his underwear, bulging from the strain of his swelling member. "Indeed, I do," he said as he removed the last of his clothing. His urge was to go to her, but something told him to wait and let her crave his newfound asset.

"Oh, Paco, what a *grande pene* you have." She looked up at Niels, her eyes brimming with a look of joyful naughtiness, of one used to getting her way. Nina kicked off her high heels and then extended her hand, and Niels assisted her to her feet. As she began to undress, her mouth drew together in a catlike smile.

* * *

Nina's head rested on Niels's shoulder as she slept. They lay naked in bed as sunlight peeked through a crack in the heavy curtains. Niels was awake, but he was in no hurry to get up. Nina's breast rested on his chest, the swell of her hip nestled in his rib cage, and her thigh grazed the side of his leg. Even asleep, a vibration of energy came off Nina's body, as if she was on twenty-four alert.

Last night they did it in multiple positions, all taking Niels to places he had never been. Nina was almost a contortionist with the manner in which she could position her legs and arch her back. It had been quite an education for Niels.

Niels raised his head over Nina's to the clock on the nightstand. It was 1:30 p.m. He laughed to himself, never in his life had he slept this late. Previously six thirty was considered sleeping in. And when he went birding, he was often up by four in the morning, the time he and Nina finally had called it an evening. It came over Niels that he was very much looking forward to birding tomorrow with Federico at Ebro Delta. This seemed to be one part of who he used to be that still remained strong. He had no idea why that was, and he had little interest in analyzing it.

Nina stirred and rolled onto her back, her eyes flickering open.

"Good morning," Niels whispered.

"Hello." Nina reached her hand down to his private parts, immediately sending a jolt through him. "I see you cannot get enough," she said as she rubbed the base with her fingers.

Niels felt as if he might explode. He reached over and placed his hand on her thigh and then worked his way up slowly. Again he felt a vibration of sexual energy between them. They were feeding off each other.

Niels rolled over on top of Nina. He entered her as her back arched up, her gasping breath hot. He began slowly and increased the pace until he was thrusting with a controlled fury. "Ooh, ooh, ooh," he uttered as her fingers kneaded the small of his back. They moved in unison, rising and descending like an experienced dance couple who knew the other's move before one made it. Nina writhed and moaned during multiple orgasms. He felt like the captain of a great sexual vessel that had been designed to his specific demands—a feminine body with long supple legs and a torso with bulges and swells in all the proper places.

Afterward they lay in bed, spent and so very satisfied. "Paco, you are King Kong," Nina said, her elbow cocked, her head resting in the palm of her hand.

"And that would make you Fay Wray."

"My grandmother knew her," Nina said with an "it is true" expression on her face.

"Your grandmother got around," Niels said with a hint of disbelief in his tone.

"You don't believe?" Nina said, sitting up. "I will prove it to you."

"Really?" Niels said as he turned on his side and faced Nina.

"At my loft where I paint, I have a storage trunk full of old photographs." Nina swung her feet around in a swift, effortless movement, sat on the side of the bed, and stretched her arms over her head. She reminded Niels of a graceful mute swan he once saw stretching its neck and wings before it took flight from a pond. She looked over her shoulder. "Come. We get dressed, and I show you."

Niels wasn't sure what it meant that she was taking him to her place. But he had a feeling that many a lover had never been there—her private sanctuary where she painted and rested from the chaos of her world.

Nina's loft was across the city on the top floor of an eight-story building. Spires and arches were integrated with more modern additions of glass-enclosed balconies with black iron trim.

The bottom floor of Nina's place had a comfortable-looking sofa with three large squishy cushions, a braided rug that complemented the hardwood floor. On the walls hung bright landscape paintings, and at the far end, there was a brick fireplace with a stone hearth. Niels had expected a sleeker, more modern look with abstract art. "Let me show you the upstairs," Nina said as she gripped the handrail of a wrought iron spiral staircase.

"You don't show it to many people, do you, Nina?" Niels lifted his chin toward the loft.

Nina's eyes had a shy, inquiring glimmer as though he had uncovered a well-kept secret. She lifted her eyebrows as a smile formed in the corner of her mouth before she turned back and headed up the steps.

The loft was a spacious, cantilevered area. Light flooded the room from two corner windows that ran the length and more than half the width of their walls. Along the third wall, which was windowless, there were stacks of paintings in a corner, a workbench, shelves stuffed with art books and painting supplies, and an old steamer trunk. In the middle of the room, there was an easel with a painting in progress of a beach scene.

Nina bent down on one knee, grabbed the trunk's leather handle, and lifted the creaky top. "Now you will see," she said as she removed dusty accordion folders teeming with old letters, a green vase, and a cracked and peeling leather album. "Yes, here it is."

Nina took a rag off her workbench, cleaned the dust from the cover, and then opened it. There were old black-and-white photos glued to the page. Below each were the names of people. At the top of the page was the year, 1931. Nina leafed through until she came to 1934. At the bottom of a page was a photo of two women and a man sitting at a table of an outdoor bistro. The inscription read, "Marne, Fay Wray, Pablo—París, Francia."

"Look," Nina said with a trill of excitement in her voice, "I kill two birds."

The picture was a bit faded, but Niels could definitely make out Picasso in a beret, his formable countenance unmistakable. Nina pointed to a dark-haired young woman with a glowing smile directed at Picasso, who was sitting in the middle. "My *abuela*, Marne." She slid her finger to Picasso and said, "What did I tell you?" She then scrolled over to the other woman, her brunette hair parted down the middle and tipping at the end in curls resting on her shoulders. Her expression was gay and light as if she were just stopping by to say hello. "Fay Wray," she said in a triumphant tone, "just like I tell you, Paco."

Niels had questions to ask about these three individuals, but his new navigational system instructed him to say little and keep her guessing. "Fascinating," he said as he looked up, surveying her loft. "This is different than I had expected."

Nina studied Niels for a moment, the eyes squinting like a huntress taking aim at her prey. The eyebrows lifted, and a smile creased her cheeks. "You expected what, Paco?" she said with a light laugh. Nina tapped her foot on the ground. "Here I paint my stories." She tilted her head toward the window. "Out there I take life as it comes to me." There was an edge of fierceness in her voice when she emphasized *take*.

The painting in progress was of a barefoot girl in a long frock dress with wide, full sleeves, and a soft sash around her waist. She was standing at an easel and facing the sea. The backdrop of water and sky was incomplete, but her clothing indicated this girl was from the past.

"How do you find your inspiration?"

"For that," Nina said as she came over, "stories my grandmother told me of her childhood."

"You would have liked to have lived back then," Niels said, "is that not so?"

"Someday you will write of our time together."

"Write?" Niels had never written anything other than technical papers for work and notes from birding.

Nina looked out the long window, the mountains in the distance undulated across the horizon like an endless line of brown humps. She turned back to Niels, her expression that of calm appraisal. "You see things, Paco." She fluttered her hands in the air as though she wanted to change the subject, as if she had had enough of the seriousness. "Now what shall we do with the rest of our day before the Count steals you away."

Nina decided on a walk through a nearby neighborhood with tree-lined streets of moderate-sized stone houses, each with a well-manicured yard and many with gardens of colorful flowers and small shrubs. Nina was quiet on the walk, other than a comment now and then on architectural style or gardening.

Later they had an early dinner at a restaurant near Niels's hotel, and after that, Nina said she would call when he returned from birding. From the time they had left her loft, her manner was somewhat restrained, as though she wanted some space between them. Niels wondered if his intuitive observation that she didn't bring many people to her painting loft had caught her off guard, possibly revealing something about herself that only her subconscious had been aware of. And now Niels wondered what machinations were processing in that intriguing mind of hers.

Back in his hotel room, Niels packed a knapsack with a rain poncho in case they met inclement weather, a small digital camera, a notebook, binoculars, and a handheld spotting scope.

Unlike many of his fellow birders, especially the less experienced, Niels didn't believe in a lot of gear. He liked to travel light. Some birders lugged around large cameras with an awkward tripod, soft-pack coolers with food and drink, and heavy, custom-made binoculars.

Just like when he traveled, Niels believed in birding with little excess. And now here in Barcelona with Nina, he applied the same discipline.

* * *

The city was dark and silent as though it was doing penance after another late night. Niels stood outside the hotel's circular drive.

A dim light emerged down the boulevard, growing larger as it neared until the sleek outline of the Count's Bentley emerged.

The driver stowed Niels gear in the trunk and opened the back door. A form in the shadows leaned its head forward. The Count's profile was faintly illuminated in the weak light. Even in silhouette there was an air of the aristocracy about him—the prominent forehead, wide and high, the finely turned nose, and the chiseled sweep of high cheekbones.

"Are you ready to bird, my friend?" There was a tone of anticipation in the voice, a birder's voice of optimism that said, "We are in this together." Niels sensed that there would be no mention of the fiesta or his high jinks. Today was all about birding.

"Greatly looking forward to it," Niels said as he sat behind the driver and across from the Count in the spacious backseat. It reminded him of a very small but exclusive men's club with a mahogany minibar and the scent of leather upholstery that brought to mind money—old money.

The car accelerated, and the lights of the city flickered into the backseat, lighting up the Spaniard's face for a moment before it returned to the shadows. "The drive is normally four hours, but with our early departure, we will make it in a little over three." Federico's voice was smooth and confident.

"Wonderful."

"Would you like some coffee?" Federico removed a thermos from a cabinet in the minibar to his left.

"Yes, thank you."

The Count poured coffee into two white porcelain cups with pink flamingos etched on the surface of each. "What may I put in your coffee?"

"A little cream, please." Niels took his cup and nodded a thank-you and raised it toward Federico. "It's always a good sign when someone I am birding with for the first time—" Niels shrugged his shoulders as if to indicate he was not too serious. "And they offer a cup of coffee adorned with birds as beautiful as flamingos."

A sliver of a grin formed in the corner of Federico's mouth as he took a hesitant sip. "It is also a good sign," he said through a smile, "when someone notices the flamingos."

Ebro Delta was a vast water land of marsh and meadows flush with a variety of birds. The Count had an extra pair of wading boots, and they spent half the day on the marsh edge and the other half inland with a guide. What a day. They saw glossy ibis, little crake, black-necked grebe with gorgeous yellow ear tufts, and so many others that Niels couldn't remember the last time he had taken such copious notes. One group of birds Niels would never forget, a colony of pink flamingos wading along the edge of the marsh. "They are *magnifico*, Federico. Magnifico," Niels had said. And to Niels's joy they began moving around in a synchronized way like a well-trained marching band, bobbing their heads in unison and looking quickly to the left and then right. What a sight.

Then a big male displayed his wings and began strutting around. "That is his mating dance," Federico said. "He is trying to impress a *certain* female."

Federico was an experienced birder, and the two exchanged birding stories that spanned many years and places. The Spaniard—Niels liked that assignation since this suave, sophisticated man epitomized the old world Spanish aristocrat—had been all over Europe and Asia and recently had returned from Suriname and raved, "I saw the exotic, such as an Amazon parrot to a rare glimpse of a tody-flycatcher."

They birded until dusk, and the limo did not return to the hotel until after midnight. Niels thanked the Count "for a day I shall never forget" and went straight to his room, tired but with a sense of well-being. During the day of birding, it came over Niels that the experience was different than any other birding day he could remember. Yes, he saw some birds he had only seen pictures of, but it was more—how he perceived the birding experience while he was at it. In the past Niels took a calm, subdued approach. Spotting a great find was an inward joy, but today it had more a sense of "Aha, another one" as he fervidly took notes describing what he had seen.

Sitting upright in bed, Niels went over his notes, and he was struck by a new twist to his writing style that he just now was aware of. "A glossy ibis spotted at 7:03 p.m.—Reddish brown body and shiny green wings." This notation was normal, but what followed was a new twist. "The bird took flight, its long imperial neck stretched out as though trying to kiss the horizon flushed pink as all around dusk fell over the land." He remembered Nina's words that someday he would write. It seemed that day was now.

Niels went to his laptop on a desk in the sitting area and began typing. He wrote for an additional forty-five minutes with a good portion about Federico.

> He has the look of Euro playboy with his perfectly golden tan and wavy dark hair, but on further inspection, one sees the good breeding in the perfect English spoken with a trace of an upper-class British accent, the chauffeured car with all the accoutrements, and the unmistakable air of one who was raised with a silver spoon in his mouth. A man who knows who he is and where he came from, a man who is perfectly content with his life of leisure.

Niels went on to describe what a fine companion the Spaniard made and how much each had enjoyed the other's company. And he also noted Federico's implication in regard to the mating dance of the flamingo. *These Spaniards do not miss much*, he thought. *They are very good, metaphorically speaking.* It was sort of similar to what Niels had done when he had been observing strangers on airplanes and comparing them to birds, but with one difference. Federico had made an acquaintance the subject he was comparing the bird to by putting emphasis on one word—*certain,* as in "certain female."

As he lay in bed, drifting toward sleep, Niels thought about how a month ago he would have thought of the Count as a Euro ne'er-do-well. Now he saw him as a charming, roughish Spaniard whom destiny had bestowed good fortune upon and was, as Nina would say, taking life as it came to him.

* * *

The next week was spent much as before, sightseeing around Barcelona, taking in the colors and history. It was a city that blended sleek modern architecture all the way back to medieval—basilicas, fortresses, and gargoyles. Much like Nina, he found this old city unfathomable and intriguing.

Included each day was an afternoon respite in a tapas bars. Federico and Niels also took another jaunt bird-watching to a different locale. It was not as vast or diverse as Ebro Delta, but it was still a splendid time. He would wine and dine with Nina too. Sometimes it was just the two of them. Sometimes she brought along a companion, either Aristo or her cousin, Carlos. Sometimes Nina would spend the night with Niels, and sometimes she would not.

The sex with Nina remained a newfound pleasure, but he realized how new this all was to him—his unyielding attraction to Nina. He tried to remain vigilant in checking his emotions. Though he didn't show it, he seemed nearly addicted to not only the sex but her company too. And when Aristo was with them, Niels had a sense of distrust, as if he were not in on everything. It wasn't that he didn't like Aristo. He was fine company, but he didn't trust him. It was more a quick glance they exchanged, a knowing look of old lovers. Was he imagining this, or were they still going at it? Or was there someone else that Aristo knew about? Would he share a good laugh with Nina about the naïve Americano? Quite possibly. The thought ransacked a new sensation through Niels's corporeal being—jealousy. *Told you so, Niels.*

It seemed hard to fathom that she was carrying on with another man, juggling two lovers while making each one think he was special, or possibly the other one was in on her charade. How could she do all that and paint? It didn't seem possible. But maybe this other man spent time at her place, and she painted during breaks. Niels had never been in her bed, always the one at his hotel.

Niels's leap of intuition came to him as he wrote in a journal that he had begun the evening after he had birded with the Count. He had never thought like this before, but he found by writing out, or more precisely typing his thoughts, it took him to a new level of consciousness. His journal entry read,

> Is Nina seeing another man? I wonder how she could physically do it, for the two of us go at it with vigor. But I sense that she possesses an unquenchable appetite that's so opposite from my wife, for whom sex seemed like a martial duty, no more, no less. I should have told you so, Laura.
>
> Sex with my wife had been a one-trick pony, once a week. Wham, bam, thank you, ma'am. Man on top, woman on bottom. Same time, same place next week. Back then I never thought much about it. We had sex every Saturday morning, and I had been under the impression I had been enjoying myself.
>
> After sex with Nina, I realize my marital intercourse had been passé, old-fashioned. I do wonder what my wife would have thought if I had tried any of Nina's moves on her. Possibly suggesting that she lean against the bedpost, spread her legs, and let me enter her from the rear. To fuck the living bejesus out of my wife. My goodness, did I just really write that? She wouldn't have known what to make of my proposal, but would she have done it? Could Niels Pettigrew and his wife have broken out of their old routine and found pleasure in discovering the secrets of each other's body?
>
> Anyway, I don't have any concrete evidence on Nina's unfaithfulness toward me. But would it really be unfaithfulness? We are not married. I am using my old value system to judge her, but I can't help it. In any event, I cannot stop my suspicions. After dinner tonight when it was just the two of

> us, there was something in her eyes when she had said, "Paco, tonight I will spend at my loft." She had laughed an overly bawdy laugh and said. "I need some rest from you, big boy." The actress in her had revealed herself.

The following morning and two days before he was to depart for home, Niels awoke early and decided to change the routine. Nina had told him that she enjoyed painting at sunrise, finding inspiration from the morning light. He would walk across town to Nina's and surprise her. The old, nagging part of him told him it was wrong to spring himself on her unannounced. But the old Niels would have never gotten this deeply involved with her to begin with. The other voice told him to throw caution to the wind, and like a good birder on a private mission to uncover some secret mating ritual of a rare, secretive bird, Nina *de aves raras*.

He wasn't sure what to expect, and that only added to his jangling nervousness. Would he be met by anger at his unexpected arrival, or would she be glad to see him and offer him her bed? Or would he find another man there? And if he did, how would he react? Poorly. Very poorly.

The walk across town took more than an hour, and Niels enjoyed watching the city wake from its slumber. He took his birding scope and stopped near a small park where he spotted a peregrine taking flight from a rooftop. When pigeons that were nesting in attic louvers flew toward the park, the peregrine dropped into a swift, steep dive, sunk its talons into an unsuspecting victim, straightened in midair, and flew off. Never had Niels witnessed such a scene in an urban environment, a city with a bird of prey.

Along the edge of a park, vendors were setting up their food stands. Shop owners were sweeping off the front walks, but few people were out, offering a different perspective of quiet solitude. Niels felt attuned to the environment as though he had an internal stethoscope listening to the city's heartbeat.

When he arrived at Nina's building, Niels took a moment to catch his breath and steady his nerves. The walk had invigorated his courage to see this through. A part of him craved Nina all the while, and another told him to reveal nothing if he found what he hoped he would not find.

He took the elevator up to the eighth floor. Nina's front door was ajar, and he peeked in. The downstairs was empty, and he stepped in and quietly went up the spiral staircase to the loft. No one was there. Niels was on high alert, like a spy on a mission to uncover the truth about a double agent who was suspected of high treason.

Niels noted that the painting of the girl at her easel on the beach appeared completed. The sky and water glistened in muted hues of blue, green, and red that added a new depth to the girl in her frock dress. He studied the painting closely and noted her sphinx-like expression added an inexplicable charm one could interpret many ways. Niels thought of her as an old soul who was wise in the ways of life and held her true and deep emotions close. The girl's drawing was a twin of herself standing at her easel and facing the sea. In the right corner was Nina's signature in black sepia, and in the left was the title, "Doppelganger."

Back downstairs Niels headed stealth-like down a narrow hallway toward Nina's bedroom. His knees were a bit shaky, and his heart pounded in his chest. He didn't believe he was really doing this. He stopped for a moment and steadied himself. *Think like a birder, and stay strong.*

The door was closed, and he wasn't sure what to do next when he heard a familiar sound. It was like a pigeon cooing but with inflections rising and lowing as if the bird was in distress. But Niels knew it was not distress but the unbridled passion of Nina de la Cerda. He wanted to run out of there and never see her two-timing face again—the bitch, the slut. *Told you so, Niels.*

He spat that little voice from his mind and gathered himself. Damn it, he would see this through. Niels adjusted his eyepiece of his scope to a forty-five-degree angle. Then he carefully opened the door just enough to place the scope in the opening. He turned the focus wheel until things became clear. Nina was riding atop a scruffy, common-looking fellow. The short, muscular body and wild thrash of hair confirmed that it was Enrico with the pirate's gleam in his eyes, the owner of the dinted and dinged wreck of a car.

They were grinding away across the width of a massive king-size bed. It surprised Niels that she was getting down with this rapscallion, and then it didn't. Nothing about her should surprise him at this point. He felt betrayed and all alone in the world at the sight of this, but he needed to keep himself together and not panic with some childish display.

A cold shudder swept through Niels when Nina stopped and took a sniff, bringing to mind a wild animal picking up a foreign scent. She turned and stared right at the scope. Niels kept it there, unable to move or think.

A faint thought whisked by that reminded him of birding in a new and exotic land and waiting for the next move of Nina de aves raras.

She started again but more slowly, her eyes on the scope, her lips twisted in a devilish grin of a disobedient child. She increased her movement and then began rocking back and forth, bending her back, lost in the rapture of the moment. Niels removed his scope and left the apartment.

On the walk back to his hotel, Niels had to stop a couple of times and gather himself. The analytical part of him was not surprised by what he had witnessed and had essentially predicted. He should have expected it. But the single man out on his own for the first time was hurt, disappointed, confused, and all the other things that come over a lover who thinks he has been done wrong. It came over him how little he knew of women, especially one as beguiling and complex as Nina.

Down a narrow side street lined with trees and green shrubs, Niels came upon a courtyard with a small fountain in the middle. People were leisurely browsing the wares set up in the front of an art shop and antique store. Past the courtyard the street narrowed again, and two women were shouting at each other across balconies. Below them, two old men wearing berets sat on a stoop and talked quietly. As Niels passed, they looked up and nodded a hello and went back to their conversation.

Everything seemed foreign and strange, and part of him ached to get home. He could do that. He could check out of his hotel and go to the airport and fly back to Philadelphia.

No, not yet. He need not rush into anything. If he stayed, what would he do if Nina contacted him? He needed to let her know how betrayed he felt and tell her never to contact him again. Or should he act if nothing had occurred, as if he had never been there and allow himself the opportunity of another chance to copulate the living bejesus out of her? He wondered if *copulate* had a verb form.

The thought of sex with Nina stirred a wrinkle of desire that grew as his carnal thoughts mushroomed. He needed to get to his room and his journal.

Niels spent an hour and a half writing in his laptop every lurid detail and his conflicting thoughts about what he had witnessed. The process helped him clear his mind and come up with a strategy. He would not contact Nina, but if she contacted him, he decided he would act as if nothing had happened.

The rest of it he would play by ear. One other thing he noted in his journal.

> It comes as a surprise to me that much like at work, here in Spain in my personal life, I am able to compartmentalize different aspects of it. The pain Nina caused I have stored away into a little vault in the back of the attic. The joy and pleasure of being in her company and the sex are being stored front and center. And writing this all out seems to help me to assimilate my thoughts. And also I enjoy

writing. Who would have known? Ah, yes, Nina—
the inexplicable Nina.

Niels spent the rest of the day walking about the city, taking in the sites, and then eating lunch at a tapas bar where he had two tall glasses of beer that put him back in a very comfortable state of well-being.

Toward the end of his walk, he went back to the cathedral that he and Nina had visited before he had received his contacts and new glasses. He took a seat in the last pew in the back. The breadth and scope of the intricate detail of the ceiling reminded Niels of how respectful Nina was when she was describing this marvelous structure. She, too, it seemed, was able to compartmentalize her life. Here in this beautiful church, she would never think of acting anything but the respectful artist of a great work.

He had no right to hold her to some high moral standard that his old self had lived by. Though he couldn't deny the fact, it still nagged at him. But what had been an open wound earlier today was now a scab and would soon scar. He would always remember this and learn from it in this life as a single man.

On the way back to his hotel, he realized the walking had given him a keen sense of well-being. He decided that when he got home, he would join a fitness center. He wanted to see what peak physical condition would do for his mental well-being and also how it would affect his newfound hobby—sport fucking.

He had heard that term *sport fucking* years ago at an insurance convention. A sales rep from another firm had drunk too much and made a fool of himself by recalling a conquest the night before to Niels and some other men. He concluded his talk by saying, "Ain't nothing in the world sweeter than a good sport fuck." Niels remembered how appalled he was as the other men laughed in a ribald, frat-boy manner, only adding to the bad taste in his mouth. His old self had found the term abhorrent, but now he saw some humor in it, though he would keep it to himself. Yes, he would start keeping many things to himself.

Niels went back to his room and took a nap. He had a dream in which Laura came back to life and flew to Barcelona. She found Niels having drinks with Enrico and Nina at a tapas bar. Each man had his arm around Nina, and they were kissing her neck as she laughed with hedonistic pleasure. "Niels," Laura called in a meek voice, "I am back." Niels turned and saw his wife standing so alone and frightened among a crowd of men arguing about soccer and Picasso all at once. They were intense, the veins of their necks pulsating. Niels shook his head at his wife and hollered, "Go back. Do not ruin it for me, Laura. Go!" Laura, her once stoically strong expression now that of unimaginable defeat, melted into the floor until she was gone.

Niels woke with a start. An ebb of sadness heaved in his chest. He sat up and shook his head. "No," he said aloud.

In his newly constructed being, he saw his marriage as stifled and restricted. He was still nineteen when he had met Laura, who was nearly twenty-one and years more assured. She had set her sights on him and won him over, not by gushing and fawning over him, but by showing a restrained interest and asking him to attend a youth ministry meeting. "We're a low-key group that you will be comfortable around." It was as if right from the start she had figured him out as a quiet, shy boy who needed guidance on finding the right path in life—her path. And once she discovered his passion for birding, Laura joined his bird-watching group and quickly learned the basic lingo and nuisances of birding.

Niels realized now that he had agreed to join Laura's church group at school in hopes of finding fellow students who weren't interested in carousing and hell-raising to all hours. He had no strong religious beliefs. His mother had been a churchgoer, but she allowed Niels to stop attending when he turned sixteen.

His main objective was to find a girl who would take things slow, a girl he could become comfortable with. And he thought he had found her in Laura, but in a way she had fooled him. She was more manipulative than any of the others in her own subtle way. Laura took his nascent beliefs on religion and molded him into her ideal husband—or so she thought. So did Niels to some degree.

After college Niels embarked on life like a horse with blinders, Laura handling the reins and reinforcing her belief in a prim and proper life, a life of abstinence from impropriety.

As he looked back now from the lens of his Spanish adventure, his seemed like a life bereft of fun. He had to admit that he had felt a sense of reward in volunteer work for their church, but he never got much out of attending church services. But it was easier to go and pretend interest than disappoint his wife. Now he wondered what he had been thinking.

It had been a life with Laura managing the house and their social life with flawless efficiency, and Niels likewise managed in business. It had all seemed so appropriate at the time, but it struck deep in the core that here in Spain was the first real fun in this life of Niels Pettigrew. Inhibitions had been tossed away with all the old beliefs in one fell swoop as if tossing out old furniture and redecorating with a newer, sleeker, shinier style.

He was no longer the man his wife had married. He had nothing to feel guilty about. She was dead, and he was alive. And by golly, he was going to take from this life what it offered him, scars and all.

Chapter 8

"Hello, Paco, did you have a good day birding about the city?"

Niels stopped in his tracks. He turned over his shoulder to the sound of Nina's voice. It seemed to float through the traffic of people coming and going in the hotel lobby directly to him. He found her sitting in the same chair in the alcove off the lobby that he had tried to read John Muir in, but to no avail.

Niels walked over. "Yes, this morning I saw a peregrine swoop down off a rooftop and snatch a pigeon out of midair. I learned much about birds of prey in Barcelona."

She raised her eyebrow and looked at him as if to say, "Touché." "Oh, Paco, you are learning."

"As I said before, you have done an excellent job of corrupting me." Niels looked down on Nina. She had on a lavender cashmere sweater and short skirt. The curves of her hips and breasts and the delineations of muscle in her long legs nearly took his breath away. She would make a fine subject for one her paintings—the beautiful vampish woman of mystery. A wave of sexual desire washed away any lingering pangs of jealousy or hurt from her romp with Enrico. Niels craved her, but he needed to show little.

She leaned back, smiling and appraising. "I do what I can." Nina tilted her head, her alluring dark eyes taking in the measure of the man before her. "Let us not banter, Paco," she said as she raised her chin in the general direction of the bar. "Buy me a drink." She nodded as if she was agreeing with herself. "On the patio in the shadows and light before our last night together."

* * *

"Sangría para la dama y la cerveza roja para mí."

"Sí, señor." The waiter tilted his head toward Niels and darted away toward the bar.

Nina sat back in her chair and crossed her legs, the supple thigh muscle undulating in a sweep to her knee. "Paco, I am impressed with your Spanish."

Niels lifted his gaze from her tantalizing legs. "The tapas bars," he said with a grin. "I listen, I learn."

Their drinks arrived. Nina had sangria, and Niels had a red beer in a tall glass. Niels raised his glass. "To our last night." He didn't know why it was their last night or why she had ended up with Enrico, but he would show no emotion, no concern.

Nina clinked his glass and took a swallow, her eyes remaining on Niels. "We had a good time, no?"

"Indeed, we did." Niels steadied his gaze on Nina. He would hold this for as long as she liked. He would show her nothing but an indifferent calm.

"Do you like your new self, Paco?" Their eyes remained locked.

"Very much. And which of yourselves do you like the best?"

"There are many parts to me, Paco." She paused for a moment, and her gaze intensified. "I do not analyze myself, I live, and I take—"

Niels interrupted. "Life as it comes to you."

Nina smiled her secret smile. "Ars longa vita brevis."

"My Latin is a little rusty," Niels said.

"It means, 'Art is long, but life is short.' We must seize the day."

"Carpe diem," Niels said.

Her smile faded, and an expression of unbridled honesty took its place. And for the first time, Niels saw behind the mask a look that said "This is who I am."

Nina placed her thumb and forefinger on the stem of her glass, raised it, and held it in front of her as if she was considering her next move, considering how much of herself to reveal. "In my art, I look to the past."

"In your art," Niels said, "you escape." He leaned forward, his eyes intently on her.

Nina stared into her glass of wine. "In life I look forward, always forward."

She looked up at Niels, and in her eyes he saw the sphinx-like expression of the girl with the old soul in the old-fashioned frock dress, painting her doppelganger into perpetuity. And then he remembered that she had gained her inspiration for that painting from stories her grandmother had told her. She put down on canvas a time she wished she had lived in again and again so that in her art she could live during that period of time forever. *Art is long.*

The sounds of chairs scraping the floor drew Nina's attention away for a moment as the only other couple on the patio got up and departed. Nina nodded good evening to them and then turned her attention back to Niels. "You are—" She fluttered her hand in the air. "What is the expression? Ah, yes. You are *figuring me out*, Paco."

Niels shrugged his shoulders slightly, his head tilting to the side, his gaze steady on Nina.

She said, "I see it in those dark-blue eyes of yours. Beautiful eyes searching for my soul."

A popping sound was followed by the rope of lights along the top edge of the wall going out. Nina's form was a shadow in the faint light coming from the lounge.

The shadow said, "Aristo and I are leaving for Greece tomorrow."

"Aristo?" This woman was full of surprises, and Niels was more than a little curious to inquire how this came about. Instead he kept his relentless gaze on the shadow. "Are you looking forward to it?"

"We are going to a villa overlooking the Aegean where we will paint."

"Marvelous," Niels said in a tone that said "Case closed."

The waiter scurried out, looking around in the darkened space. "Sin luce," he said, scrolling his finger toward the wall. Niels took a long swallow of his beer, finishing it. "No problemático," he said to the waiter. He raised his empty glass. "Uno mas."

Nina leaned forward and put her hand on Niels's cheek. "Are you angry with me, Paco?"

Her touch felt like that of an old friend, a fond friend about to say good-bye. "Quite the opposite," he said as he placed his hand on hers.

Nina brought her face close to Niels. Her breath smelled of sweet wine. Desire infiltrated his nostrils. "I have one last favor to ask of you," she said.

Niels took her chin in his hand and stroked it. "After dinner we will go to my room." He leaned over the table and kissed her softly on the lips. He whispered in her ear, "And you may have your way with me."

"Hah," Nina laughed as she leaned back. "Paco, you have intuition and spirit." They paused for a moment as Niels was served his beer. "We will have magnificent last night." Nina strung the word out in a singsong manner—*mag-nifff-eeee-cent.*

* * *

Nina and Niels untangled after a mutual climax. As she rested her head on his shoulder, he realized that tonight was the last time he would feel her velvety skin or enjoy her company. Part of him would miss her. Another part realized that any other option was impossible.

"What are you thinking, Paco?"

"Why me?"

Nina ran her hand under Niels's chin. "When I first saw you, I knew I must have this man." She arched her brow as if she was considering her words. "You were so sad-looking, but beneath the sadness I saw passion in those beautiful, so very beautiful eyes of yours."

"On a stranger's face on an airplane?"

"Your face was not that of a stranger," she said, placing her hand on Niels's chest, "but that of one who had not found his inner self. I saw a soul simpatico." Nina laughed at her words. "And for a brief moment, I saw a handsome, very handsome man behind the big glasses and sadness."

There were so many things Niels wanted to say, but he held his words, his eyes staring into hers, saying farewell with an edge of sexual desire.

"We were good together, no?"

"Yes," Niels said, "damn good."

Nina propped her elbow and rested her chin in her palm. "So you return to Philadelphia." She ran her hand through Niels's bristly head of hair. "It will be different from before."

"Much different. I am different," Niels said. "It is entirely your fault," he said in a teasing tone.

"I revel in my creation," Nina said as she leaned over and kissed him. She then looked at him as one does an old friend never to be seen again. "One last thing."

"Yes, Nina," Niels said. "I am listening."

"Look forward, Paco. Always look forward."

Chapter 9

Niels sat in his window seat as the passengers filed by. He removed from his carry-on the biography of John Muir, determined to begin reading it after the plane took off. When the last passenger had boarded and the door was secured, it came over Niels that he had the row to himself. It had been a little more than two weeks since Nina had sat down next to him on the flight over. It seemed like years to Niels, wonderful years—with a few hard lessons learned. It felt as if his life had slowed down while in Barcelona.

He had recorded every detail of his trip in his journal. He wrote in it each evening, or if he was with Nina, he'd write in the morning when he was alone. It now seemed as much a part of his life as birding. An entry the morning before departure read,

> I will need to figure out a plan about meeting women. Not any type of women but ones who are into bedroom romps. There is a whole new world out there that I never considered before, and I owe it to Nina for showing it to me. With distance, I see her fling with Enrico was simply that, nothing more than a physical act from which she derived pleasure. I must keep that in mind in my future

dalliances and work out a plan how to make it come to fruition.

There were other things to consider back home. While in Barcelona, he had received an e-mail from his attorney about a settlement from the airlines in regard to Laura's death. Niels said he would call when he returned home. But it was simmering in his mind that the offer was not enough. There was no proof of pilot error, just the bad luck of the plane being in the wrong place at the wrong time. But Niels would still crunch out some numbers, draw up an actuarial table, and decide from there.

As the flight attendant whisked down the aisle and asked passengers to raise their seats, Niels thought about how he had always taken pleasure in the minutia of numbers and probability and all the rest that entailed his occupation. Now he wasn't so sure. He would see how it went.

One thing he was sure of was that he would join a health club, which might present opportunities to meet women while he was getting in shape. He also wanted to learn how to cook, and as the plane began taxiing down the runway, he thought he would try to read this book in his lap. Hello, John Muir.

* * *

As the US coastline came into view, Niels closed the book. He hadn't gotten very far. He had made three attempts to read it, and each time he couldn't find any interest in a man whom he had considered the embodiment of an American hero. Now he wondered how the man could have possibly lived in the wilderness alone for months on end.

Something had emerged while he was in Spain, and Nina had triggered it. Or perhaps the real trigger was Laura's death, and Nina only pulled it. In any event, there would be time to sort all these things out and to see what the future held.

Niels saw Andrea in a cluster of people waiting for arriving passengers. She was looking for Niels, but at the same time he saw that she was thinking of other things. The poor kid's life had been turned upside down with the death of her mother, and she looked to be in need of some family time.

The squawking blare of the PA system announcing departures and arrivals and the bustling tension hanging in the air brought a sense of edgy anticipation to the forefront of Niels's mind. "Andrea," Niels said as he waved to his daughter. A look of recognition came over her as she looked past Niels, searching for his voice. "I'm here, honey," Niels said as he walked up to her.

"You're not wearing your glasses," she said as she embraced her father in a big hug. This surprised Niels, for they had always been reserved about showing any sign of affection in public. Why that was he didn't really know other than they were not a touchy-feely people. Andrea stepped back. "Dad, you look so different."

"I lost my glasses and got contacts and a new pair of glasses."

"You look handsome, Dad."

"Oh, it's the same old me."

Andrea studied her father, sensing that there was more going on than contact lens. "You must tell me all about Spain. Your e-mails were so brief," she said, scrunching up her face in an inquisitive manner.

"Oh, were they?" Niels said. "Let us get my baggage, and I will tell you all about it." Of course, Niels had no intention of telling his daughter that he was no longer the man he used to be, that he had had a wild fling with an exotic Spanish artist, that he fully intended to have more, or that he enjoyed alcoholic beverages—all in due time.

On the ride home, Andrea asked Niels if he meet any interesting people. He did tell her about birding with Federico and offered a sanitized version of the fiesta at Aristo's estate. He emphasized his walks about the historic districts and birding in the city. "I owe it to you, dear," Niels said as he turned to his daughter behind the wheel of her car. "If you hadn't convinced me to take this trip … well, it was a wonderful tonic."

Andrea glanced at her father, a squint in her eyes. "I am so glad." Her voice had a quiver in it that told Niels she had not recovered. He, on other hand, felt like his marriage to Laura was in another life. He was another man who had returned home eager to take each day as it came.

As Andrea's car pulled into Niels's neighborhood, all appeared similar, but it was as if he perceived the place through a different lens. It was like returning to a birding spot after years away. The stately, well-manicured homes and foliage enveloping the streets had always brought a sense of appreciation after business trips. He was about to arrive on his quiet street and go into his immaculate home, where his taciturn but organized wife had always waited with a dinner and a typed schedule of the upcoming weekend on his dresser.

> Friday
> 7:00 p.m. Reverend Pritchard has requested you review with him the church insurance policy.
>
> Saturday
> 7:00 a.m. Leading guided tour at Audubon.
> 10:00 a.m. Dentist appointment.
> 1:00 p.m. Clothing drive in church parking lot—volunteers needed.
> 4:00 p.m. Tea at Henderson's to brainstorm upcoming charity ball.
>
> Sunday
> 6:00 a.m. Birding at Hechsher Park
> 11:00 a.m. Church service—don't be late!

Now he wanted more than his old robotic life.

He had spent two weeks with an unpredictable woman who was anything but quiet and who gobbled up life in a chaotic, loud, abrasive style. She had turned on a pilot light inside Niels that he never knew existed.

They left the baggage at the foot of the steps and walked through the dining room, which they had rarely used. When he entered, Niels felt his wife's persona—polite and courteous but covered in a thin layer of ice—everywhere in this cold space—the double-pedestal cherry dining table with rigid high-back armchairs, ornate brass chandeliers, and an imposing credenza looming in a corner.

The chill began to lift when he entered the kitchen with granite countertops, cherry cabinets with salvaged brass handles, travertine tile floor, and adjoining breakfast nook, where he had eaten meals.

Past the kitchen was Niels's favorite room, the den, where they positioned themselves as they did after the funeral. Niels kicked off his shoes and put his feet up on the table without giving it a second thought. "How are you, honey?"

"I'll be okay, Dad." Andrea dropped her gaze as she absentmindedly gnawed on her thumbnail. It was an old childhood habit that had left her nails worn down to the nub until age sixteen when she stopped. She only reverted back when she was under stress or unhappy.

"How is work coming?"

Andrea looked up. "Oh, I got a promotion." She went on to tell with rising enthusiasm about her new responsibilities. Niels saw that her youth was an asset. She had her entire life in front of her, and soon she would be back on track. Soon she would slip back into the rhythm of her new career and unfolding life.

She was a smart, levelheaded young woman whose presence Niels had always enjoyed, a sweet, inquisitive child who had grown into a capable adult with an uncanny ability to size up a situation and find a solution. Niels thought it began with dealing with her formidable mother. Instead of resisting, she adapted and learned from her mother.

Andrea's presence removed a layer of frost from Laura's outer shell that made things more tolerable and sometimes close to joyful during the holidays. Whether cooking together in the kitchen or working on a refinishing project in the basement, afterward it seemed Laura's high-voltage tension had been downgraded, but only for a while. Soon it reemerged like a pot of boiling water that never evaporated.

As much as he now felt a sense of distain toward his wife's dominance in their relationship, Niels had accepted it without complaint. He was as much to blame as Laura, for he could have stood his ground as he did about her not interfering with his birding. He saw now that he had been lackadaisical in his development as a husband and a man, always taking the path of least resistance.

* * *

Niels returned to work on Monday. By the end of the morning, the sympathy visits under the guise of inquiring about his trip from colleagues and staff had ended, and he could catch up on his backlog. As head of the financial management department, his office was in a desirable corner location with a splendid view of downtown Philadelphia overlooking Broad Street, City Hall only a few blocks away.

He stared at a stack of folders from his right-hand man, a young actuary with great promise. In them were his travel itinerary for next month, updated actuarial tables that meant adjustments on policy standards, and all the endless changes that it precipitated.

Niels pushed the folder off to the side of his desk. He picked up his phone. "Edward, come up to my office, if you would."

Within a minute a young man of thirty dressed in a starched white shirt and a black tie sat in front of Niels's desk.

"I was just looking these over," Niels said as he tapped the folders. "By the way, congratulations on passing the casualty exams."

"Thank you, sir."

"That makes you a full-fledged actuary." Niels spun his chair around and went to the window. Ten stories below, the cars and people looked like miniature characters. He had never thought of it in that way before. "I think it is high time you were given responsibility befitting someone of your new stature here at the firm." Niels went to his desk and handed the folders save the one with his travel itinerary to young Edward.

"Really, sir?"

"We are in the business of risk management," Niels said, "and I believe you are a good risk."

Edward straightened his already rigid posture, his eyes those of one winning a big prize. "I won't let you down, Mr. Pettigrew."

"I know you won't." Niels raised a finger as if to say, "One more thing." "And this will free me up for a special project I have been contemplating."

Edward leaned forward, his gaze inquisitive. "If I may ask, what might that be, sir?"

Niels folded his arms across his chest and said, "Lifestyle changes and the effects it has on one's health, mental and physical."

* * *

As Niels returned back to his life in Philadelphia, he found some aspects of it unacceptable. He was tired of the ennui of work and its endless details, something he used to never tire of. However, he wasn't tiring of his continuation of the journal he wrote in the evening, trying to make sense of his new perceptions. The material wasn't as rich as it had been in Spain, but he recorded the day's events and made observations about the people he came in contact with.

> It has come to my attention that actuaries are a boring lot. They are almost machinelike in the dispensing of their duties, little humor about them.

> While nobody would confuse my birding friends as a wild-eyed group, they have a passion for birding that transcends words—a look of utter surprise at the sight of an unexpected bird hidden in a cluster of trees, a twinkle in the eyes at the sound of a cardinal's metallic chirp. Birders are like-minded, moderate folks whose idea of a rousing time is spending twelve hours trampling through forests, mountains—anyplace with birds.

Another new step he took was a weight lifting regimen he found online. He joined a fitness club and began weight training on numerous cable machines from lat pull-downs to curls and his favorite, the rowing machine. Every weekday morning at six, Niels began a routine that he had built up to an hour and a half. The results were encouraging. He had lost fifteen pounds, and he had begun to notice new definition in the musculature in his arms and torso. And his face was beginning to lose the puffy look as he began to see more of his youthful handsomeness return.

Niels went online and got healthy recipes and experimented. Andrea gave him a few rudimentary culinary lessons, and off he went, making stuffed peppers with chicken and brown rice, steamed vegetables, spinach salad with a honey-vinegar dressing he made up.

And then he did something that he could not have ever imagined before. He sold the dining room furniture and upholstery, hired a decorator, and converted the space into an office study. He bought a weaved carpet to soften the hardwood floor, yellow curtains with pictures of songbirds in place of the formal drapes with brass-plated rods, a corner desk set with a swivel chair with a view of a bird feeder in the side yard. On the walls were hung landscape pictures that added the finishing touches. The room felt like his and his alone.

His attorney had contacted Niels about the airline's retribution for Laura's death. They would not negotiate, and each individual was being offered the same amount—$1.5 million. The old Niels would have dug in and fought them tooth and nail. But this money was tax-free, and combined with what he had invested and saved, he had the freedom to do whatever he pleased. Niels accepted. Plus, he wanted to put all that behind him and go forward into his new life. He wasn't sure what exactly that was yet, but he would give it time.

He had yet to find an acceptable routine to meet women. Niels didn't like to drink and drive. He had heard too many MADD meeting horror stories from Laura. He could take a cab, but it struck his as desperate. In Spain, he felt comfortable in the bars, but something about Philadelphia nightlife didn't sit right. Too close to home? He couldn't put his finger on it. Something was bound to come up. But he needed it soon. His exercise routine had only increased his libido. He was downright horny.

Laura's death had freed him up from obligations to her schedule of duties. Birding took his mind off things, and he spent weekends at it either alone or with a group from the Audubon. They were a typical collection of birders, anywhere from six to ten men and women. Birders were, for the most part, a quiet, introspective lot with keen minds and a passion for discovering something rare in nature.

But in some instances, they had not been conservative enough for Laura. One year at the annual Audubon Convention at Cape May, Niels was deeply absorbed in conversation with a retired college professor who told of seeing a wattled ibis in the Ethiopian highlands. A waiter came by to take a drink order, and the professor asked Niels if he could buy him a cocktail. Niels paused for a moment, considering. Most folks were imbibing carefully, talking bird talk. *It might be fun to share a cocktail*, he had thought. Everyone seemed to be getting into the spirit of anticipation of a field trip the next day at Lighthouse Pond, where a black-necked stilt had been spotted.

Laura appeared seemingly out of nowhere. It was as if her radar had detected a *situation*. Her sharp-eyed gaze had that look as if an alarm had gone off. "We don't drink," she said to the professor. "Come, Niels. It is time for us to leave." Like an obedient retriever, Niels nodded good night and followed his wife away from temptation. Next time he was offered a drink, he would take them up on it.

* * *

Another week of getting up at five and going off to the gym and then heading to the office had provided little new material for his journal, but he kept at it and decided to include any birds he had seen during the day.

This was a change in format for Niels since Laura had always maintained Niels's bird-watching journal. For each decade there was a leather-bound notebook. She had copied Niels's notes of birds that he had spotted in the backyard and on birding jaunts. Listed in numerical order were date, time, gender, bird sounds, and other birding minutia. She had been very thorough, and Niels had appreciated the care she took inserting any pictures and accompanying typed data in cellophane sleeves. *Yellow warbler at edge of backyard pond—first sighting this spring!* Since his wife's death, the book had not seen a single entry.

Now his efforts were on his new journal that not only recorded his day but offered interpretations of what he had seen.

> Spotted red-tailed hawk from office window perched atop a building like a monarch overlooking his realm. I think the reason I have always been drawn to birding is the freedom that birds have to fly off and go wherever the currents take them.

The upcoming weekend should provide his newfound muse something of interest. Niels was very much looking forward to a Saturday birding with some fellow birders at a marsh near the Schuylkill River, one known for its migratory bird routes.

There was a rare sighting of a red-necked phalarope there, a bird that Niels had wanted to see for years. It spends nine months a year in the lower Arctic and migrates to tropical climes, which was unusual for a wader. He knew the odds of the bird still being there and of him finding it were slim. It still gave him a sense of anticipation, something that had been sorely missing from his life since Spain.

Niels had arranged to drive his car accompanied by John and Mary Shorter and Bob Mackenzie, whose wife was not into birding. Niels and Laura had been birding with the Shorters for more than ten years and even socialized on occasion. Most birders Niels knew were married, and both spouses were active, though some like Laura did it to be with their husband. Bob's situation was the exception, and he seemed almost like a bachelor, which Niels was now.

Niels pulled into the Shorter's driveway at dawn and saw Mary come out by herself. He leaned over the seat and opened the passenger door. "Where's John?"

"His father took ill," she said as she stowed her knapsack in the back. "He left last night for Jersey."

As Niels did the obligatory query about the health and well-being of John's father, his eyes were looking over the woman to his right—late thirties, brunette, with an athletic, natural look about her. She had been a member of her college swim team and had maintained an attractive figure. She wore little makeup, if any, and Niels had always found her an attractive woman; however, she seemed a bit reserved as though she was hiding something stirring below the surface. And from her he felt the charge of a heightened sense of awareness, as if she were meeting a handsome stranger for the first time.

As he drove off to pick up their other passenger, they small talked about birding mostly, but the dynamics had changed. Mary was without her husband, and Niels's wife was dead. He sensed an undercurrent of interest from Mary, as though she were looking at something unusual like a birder making a good spot. "You look so different, Niels." She studied him closely, her analytical eyes missing nothing. "No glasses, and you're letting your hair grow out."

"Oh, yes, I felt like a change." He turned to her and smiled, and in her gaze he saw something, a nascent hunger not yet discerned or understood. But it was there in her eyes even if the rest of her was unaware. Niels wished that he didn't have to pick up Bob, that it was just the two of them birding all day. He told himself to slow down and let the day unfold. He did wonder if, by the end of the day, he could call himself an adulterer. Or would only Mary be the adulterer or adulteress since she was the only one married?

Niels, Mary, and Bob met a married couple in the park's parking lot. Two other couples had canceled at the last moment. Ideas were bandied about where to bird. Bob wanted to climb up to a lookout and observe birds of prey swooping down on flocks of migrating birds, and the couple said they would join him. "Well," Niels said in a confident voice, "Mary and I will stay along the river and marsh and see what we discover." He glanced at Mary and saw in her gaze a look of approval.

They decided to meet back at noon for lunch and to exchange info on sightings before they returned for more.

Niels and Mary walked along a canal towpath, a line of trees separating them from the Schuylkill. She birded light with a small knapsack strung across her shoulders, containing binoculars and the basics.

The other couple had brought a tripod and camera and a tape recorder with birdcalls, and the husband had a large pack on his back, containing every birding gizmo. Niels got most of his joy in birding from seeing the rara avis and shooting a quick picture with his Canon 1. It was a reliable camera, and he could get off a shot when he was on the move in seconds.

Niels never wanted to dismiss the sight of any bird no matter how common, but he had a feeling that today might be special in more ways than one. Mary pointed to a great blue heron along the canal edge, standing as still as a statue. "I saw a gray heron in Spain," Niels said. "Very similar but somewhat smaller."

"You must tell me sometime about birding over there." Mary stopped when the big bird broke the water surface with its long, sharp beak and came up with a snapping turtle dangling from its end. A couple of quick snaps worked the turtle back toward its demise before it was swallowed whole. Niels and Mary snapped off some photos. "Wow," Niels said, "that was something." He turned to Mary as she was putting her tiny camera in an Altoid case. "What quality pictures do you get?"

"Good. It has point-and-shoot with zoom." Mary looked past the heron to the thick woods along its other side. "Niels, did you hear that?"

The scolding *cheh-cheh* of a bird flitting about caught Niels's ear. "Yes, a house wren. I love their song."

"There it is," Mary said in a low voice, pointing. She turned and looked at Niels. "I heard one singing at Laura's funeral." She paused and said, "It seemed so very appropriate." Mary arched her brow, her eyes impassive, but behind them was something more like a yearning.

"Yes, I heard it too." Niels's thoughts of his distress that day were presently overrun by his urge to sidle up to Mary and put his arm around her waist. But he remembered his discipline with Nina and made no such move. *Let it come*, he told himself. *Let the day bring what it may, and take what it offers.*

They decided to head into the woods and then loop around the riverbank on their way back for lunch. Before, when they were birding with their spouses, there was an easiness, a comfortableness of two couples with a common interest in one subject—birding. Niels had never thought of Mary as an object of his sexual fantasies. And he supposed she hadn't thought that with him. But now that he was a single man with a new and improved appearance and her husband was absent, she looked at him differently. Not with a flirtatious glance or comments, but there was a mutual undeniable attraction drawing them together.

Along the river, an osprey with a fish in its talons flew overhead and followed the path of the water until it disappeared into the horizon. They also saw a belted kingfisher, red-winged blackbird, and a juvenile bald eagle still growing into its plumage, its head a mixture of brown and white, its beak black. They both watched with binoculars until the eagle disappeared into a cluster of tall trees. "That was special," Mary said with an edge of excitement in her voice that he had never heard before. In the past she had always maintained a low-key tenor as she commented on birds. To Niels this had seemed proper. It fit with her job as a research scientist for a pharmaceutical company. She came across as an intelligent, no-nonsense individual who had little emotion or kept it very close. Now it seemed she was revealing another part of herself, and he found it arousing.

On the last leg along the river before they turned back on the towpath, Niels and Mary stood side by side, surveying the water. Mary saw it first through her binoculars and pointed up river. "Near the shoreline," she whispered.

Niels adjusted his lens on a bird wading, and at first he thought it a mallard until he focused in on the patch of reddish yellow on the side of the neck. "My God," Niels said, "it's a red-necked phalarope."

The bird began swimming in a small rapid circle, dipping its sharp black beak into the water. "Look at that." Niels heard the awe in his voice.

"Let's get closer," Mary said as she motioned Niels to follow. "I've read they are approachable."

They stopped no more than fifteen feet from the bird. *How beautiful and unique*, Niels thought, *with its chestnut breast and black face and a small white spot above the eye. What a magnificent creature.*

For five minutes Niels and Mary observed, taking pictures as the bird plucked its beak into the water and continued to swim in a circle. "I believe that's a female," Mary said.

"Yes, the males are not as colorful."

"Whit-whit," the bird called. "Whit-whit."

"I wonder if it has lost its migrating flock," Mary said.

"Very possible," Niels said as the bird suddenly flew off toward the south. Niels dropped his binoculars. "Well, at least it's heading in the right direction."

"I wonder," Mary said, looking up at Niels, "if it lost its mate and became disoriented."

"Huh?" Niels exchanged a quick glance with Mary. "I've never heard or read that."

"No, I haven't either," Mary said slowly as if considering. "But I wonder if their biology doesn't change when a sudden loss occurs."

At lunch at a picnic table, Niels and Mary's report on the red-necked phalarope was met with "Oh, how wonderful. Make sure to post it on the Audubon website. That's a moment you will never forget."

The others had had little luck looking for birds of prey and decided to spend the afternoon along the river while Mary and Niels would go up to higher ground.

Anxious to change their luck, the remainder of the group left Niels and Mary at the table. As they were preparing to begin their walk, Mary's cell phone beeped. She read a text message, and her expression changed from birding to business. "My husband's father had a heart attack," Mary said as she looked up at Niels. In her gaze Niels saw not a whit of distress but a keen glimmer in her eyes of an opportunity on the horizon. "He's expected to recover, but Bob will stay a few more days."

Niels exchanged a long look with Mary, a look of two people sharing a secret.

* * *

Niels dropped off Bob and had fifteen minutes to figure out a plan to get together with Mary. Maybe she would help him along. After lunch they had hiked up a switchback trail and found an overhang with a view of the valley. They decided to sit on a rock and look for birds. They spotted some, but nothing as special as the red-necked phalarope in the morning. They talked a bit about things other than birding, and Mary intimated not in what she said but what she did not say. Her marriage had plateaued. She and her husband had never had children and had recently celebrated their fifteenth anniversary with a birding trip to Puerto Rico. She told Niels about all the exotic parakeets they'd spotted. But her voice had a hollow ring to it as if she was talking about a business trip.

As Niels pulled into Mary's driveway, she looked at him, her eyes saying, "What now?" "I had a great time with you today," she said.

Niels reached his hand over and placed it on her wrist. "You were a perfect companion, Mary."

Mary laced the fingers of her free hand through Niels's and squeezed. "Would you like to come in for a drink?" Her lips twisted in a crimp of self-doubt. "Oh, I forgot you don't drink."

"Oh, I have changed my ways," Niels said. "In more ways than one."

"Really?"

"Yes," Niels said as he leaned toward her, and she met him halfway, his face in hers, strands of her hair grazing his cheek. He kissed her on the lips. She drew into him, her strong, vibrant body nestling tightly against his.

Mary asked Niels to have a seat in her den while she got out a bottle of pinot noir. He went to a comfortable-looking love seat that would hold two people just fine. Mary came over with two glasses and the wine. Niels poured and handed Mary her drink. He clinked her glass and said, "To a great day birding."

Without missing a beat, Mary said, "And to an even better evening."

Niels put his arm over her shoulder and brought her close. He kissed her neck and got a faint whiff of sweat from a day of birding mingled with her natural feminine scent. It was a devastating combination.

* * *

The jangling ring of a telephone woke Niels from a deep sleep. A light came on, and Mary swept out from under the covers, sat up naked on the side of the bed, and answered the phone on her nightstand. The call was brief. "Hello? I see. Do you want me to come up now? Okay, call when the arrangements have been made."

Mary returned to bed, her head against the headboard, her pubic hairs reminding Niels of a robin's nest. She could have been a nude model posing, a very lean and fit model at that. "John's father passed away."

They exchanged glances, and in her eyes he saw what he felt—no obligation to comment further. For a fleeting moment, a thought passed that he was not the man he used to be, but that was the way it was with him now. He felt no remorse for John's loss, only an avarice lust for a grieving man's wife. His loss was Niels's gain. He slid his hand onto Mary's thigh and slowly brought it up until his finger was inside her, stroking. Mary began breathing in heavy gasps, "Ooh, ooh."

During a cordial cup of coffee at Mary's kitchen table, neither of them spoke of the passing of John's father. Niels was surprised at Mary's nonplussed reaction, but he would not probe. He did wonder if she would want to get together with him again, but he would wait and see how she played it.

Mary took a sip of coffee and held it to her lips for a moment. "You gave me a fine education last night."

"A few things I picked up in Spain."

She placed her cup in the saucer and stared off for a moment. "Is there anything else from you I need to learn?"

"My bedroom would make a marvelous training facility."

"That sounds like a plan," Mary said, raising her foot up into Niels's crotch. "That is quite an impressive piece of apparatus you have."

Indeed, it is, Niels thought. *Indeed, it is.*

> Mary is a bit of a strange bird, almost antiseptic in her response to her husband's situation. And I noted that she never mentioned his name, John, once, always referring to him as "my husband" as if he were no more than a piece of furniture in the house that could be easily replaced.

Chapter 10

Niels received one startling piece of news from Andrea, who had been offered a position with her firm in Melbourne, Australia. It was a plum assignment, and Andrea asked her father for advice. Niels told her that although he would miss her—and he would—this was an opportunity that she could not turn down if she was serious about her career. The day Niels watched her plane take off, he had mixed feelings. He was sad to see her leave, but now he was completely free of any constraints as he was in Spain. *So now*, he thought, *time to get into the swing of things.*

A routine was established where Niels and Mary would meet every Wednesday afternoon at his place. The first time Niels offered her a glass of wine, but she said she didn't want her husband getting suspicious with her coming home with alcohol on her breath. And she didn't have a lot of time, so upstairs they went. She would arrive at four and be out the door no later than five thirty.

During pillow talk, Mary confided in Niels that her husband was fifteen years older and that his libido had descended to the point that sex was a rare event in their marriage. She considered her dalliances with Niels the fulfillment of a biological need. "And you, big fella, have an abundance to fulfill me with," she told him as she took his private part in her hand.

Mary enjoyed foreplay, and they spent a good deal of their time arousing each other with something new each week. Mary enjoyed using her tongue, licking Niels in every nook and cranny. He, on the other hand, offered pleasure with hands and fingers, starting at her toes and slowly working his way up, caressing her ankles, kneading her calves, and lingering at her sweet spot. By the time his fingers reached her nipples, Mary was in full pant.

Sex with Mary was different from the wild, passionate Nina. There was passion with Mary, but she was not passionate. Simply put, she was a horny woman who got herself off with Niels every week. There wasn't a hint of infatuation or love. No, this was, as Niels understood it, two people who had something they needed from the other.

But Niels missed the excitement of the unknown that seemed to be a part of Nina's DNA. With Mary, he knew she would arrive at his place every Wednesday at four, and soon after that, they would end up in bed. Little conversation would happen before or after, and as the weeks went on, even that lessened.

He felt trapped. His body craved the sex, but he was tired of Mary. She was a bore. So he went online and found a single's bar nearby, Mickey's Taproom. He decided that he was desperate enough to consider a cab.

Mickey's was located in a strip mall near a local college campus. The long, wide space with a high ceiling, exposed beams, and rafters was most likely a converted warehouse. Pictures and jerseys of professional athletes hung on the brick walls. There was a long bar in the front, a smaller round one in the back, and a corner alcove with a dartboard. TVs showing football games were everywhere—above the bars, along the walls, and a big screen hanging from the ceiling. *Ah*, Niels thought, *I'm in a sports bar, a first.*

There was a faint odor of stale beer and a youthful vibe about the place as college kids wearing jeans and sneakers were half-watching a game on TV and carrying on in excited, loud conversations, drinking beer from plastic cups. Niels felt as if he had invaded a kiddy room for beer drinkers.

He stood just off the double-wide entrance with its shiny brass door, U-shaped handles, and stained glass windows. He felt *so* out of place standing there in his creased slacks, polo shirt, and the tasseled loafers that he had recently purchased. Whatever was he thinking coming here?

Three empty stools at the end of the long bar seemed like a safe haven. He took a seat and ordered a draft beer.

The beer tasted stale, and drinking out of plastic didn't help. The bar was half filled with boys checking out a group of attractive coeds sitting in a booth. This was definitely a pickup place, but was it suited for a fifty-year-old man?

Niels turned to a tap on his shoulder. There stood a young fellow of college age dressed in an Eagles hoodie. He was of medium build and average size with that preppy, wise-guy aura about him. Niels knew that look well from his days at prep school.

"Excuse me," the boy said, "but do you mind settling a bet I have with my buddies?" He slung his thumb over his shoulder in the general direction of a similar clad group of guys with mocking eyes and smug smiles.

Niels realized he was the subject of some sort of college prank. "Yes, how can I be of help?"

"My buddies think—" A smile cracked the corner of the boy's mouth as he turned back to his friends who were egging him. "Come on, Johnny. I double-dog dare you." The group broke into hooting laughter.

Johnny continued, "That you're here to get laid."

Niels felt the blood rush up his neck and settle in his cheeks. He got off his stool and stood tall, his big-shouldered frame towering over his questioner. His workouts and weight loss had given him a physical presence and confidence that he hadn't felt since college. "Really, and what gave you that impression?" Niels voice had a dangerous edge to it that he had never heard before.

The wiseacre look had left the boy's face and was replaced by an *Oh, oh* expression. "I, ah—"

Niels raised his voice and looked toward his buddies. "Why don't you run along back to your friends," Niels said as he lifted his chin toward the other boys, "and I'll finish my beer and leave this place to you and your heroic friends."

Niels kept his gaze on the group of boys, who all had looked away. He turned back to his questioner. "Sound like a plan?"

"I, ah—"

"Speak up," Niels demanded.

The boy nodded his head. "Yes, sir." Slump-shouldered, he returned in defeat back to his group.

Niels sat back on his stool, finished his beer, and left but not before he turned a bone-chilling gaze on Johnny and his buds, none of whom said a peep.

That evening Niels wrote in his journal,

> Visited a sports bar near campus and learned a few things. One, college hangouts are not my cup of tea.
>
> Two, I discovered not only can I stand up for myself but I don't take shit from anyone. Who knew? Seems I'm learning something new about the new Niels Pettigrew every day.

So Niels continued his visits with Mary, and during this time he continued to get up early and go to his fitness center Monday through Friday. He had lost a total of twenty-five pounds. He had so much more energy and drive, but he found his job as an actuary stilting and boring. His young aide, Edward, had taken a great load off his plate, and Niels had started to leave work early to get in an afternoon workout either at the gym or running in his neighborhood.

He enjoyed working out in the afternoon because it lessened his guilt about enjoying a few beers before dinner in the evening. He had become a fan of Guinness and Bass ale and had recently discovered Black and Tan, which was a combination of the two.

He had also figured out where the dry cleaner was. He had become familiar with where things were stocked at his local grocery store, and he began getting his life into some semblance of order. But he wanted more. Ever since he had left that grand and high time in Spain, life seemed rather pedestrian. The sex with Mary wasn't enough. The workouts only ratcheted up his quest for an adventure of some sort.

Next week's business trip couldn't arrive soon enough, his first since Laura's death, and he was looking forward to it. Not the work, but the opportunities that it might offer.

He was to visit three of the insurance company's branch offices to reiterate the new policies in regard to various changes in risk management. In the past Niels found these trips tedious, taking him away from his number-crunching and coming as close as possible to configuring the most advantageous actuary tables for the betterment of the firm. These trips had been more a visit from a big shot at corporate headquarter than substantive.

This time—and for the first time—Niels had written a presentation for each of the three offices he would visit. He was traveling to Tampa, San Antonio, and Spokane. He had a gift for taking complex concepts and writing a clear and concise PowerPoint presentation with little difficulty.

For this trip, he conceptualized all the aspects of his subject matter and then wrote it out, incorporating personal antidotes and a history lesson to hold his audience's attention. He had actually enjoyed the exercise, finding pleasure in not only simplifying the subject but in making it a story of sorts. And to take it full circle, he wrote in his journal that he liked the idea of connecting the dots when he was writing.

Writing had always come easy to Niels. He could always whip out business letters and technical papers in no time. It was clean, professional, and concise writing that let the reader know that the author knew his field. He had transferred that talent to his daily journal, which he had named *Memoir Musings.* He expanded it with astute observations of the events or nonevents that he surmised something from.

> Kenner in accounting has that look of one who seems as though his world is falling apart. His narrowed-eyed, factoid businessman has been replaced by a look of a fearful, wondering nerd. It's not very attractive. My guess is he has some sort of problem at home with the wife—a looker—who might just have found another doghouse to play in.

In Spain, the writing was wild and wooly, and he had little problem with keeping a lively pace. Back home he found the ennui of work a challenge that sharpened his writing skills and eye for detail. But he promised himself that on this upcoming trip, he would have something of substance to enter.

* * *

The branch office in Tampa was in the business district, a short walk from Niels's hotel. During that first morning, he woke at five and worked out in the hotel's rudimentary fitness room. Unsatisfied, he took a seven-mile run around the city. His jog included a wide walkway bordering the bay, a trail through parkland, and an upscale historic neighborhood with well-manicured Victorian homes, the streets lined with mangroves. It was a good run in an attractive environment, a great way to start the day.

At nine o'clock sharp, Niels began his PowerPoint presentation. Instead of offering exclusively facts and numbers, he included examples of success stories by using the new risk management policy or RMP as he called it. Niels added a human interest touch to it by beginning with a question, "What does it take to manage risk in an uncertain world?"

He mingled his data with an allegorical tale of the risk management of an English baron in the sixteenth century and how much wheat to grow in relation to the other crops. He brought it full circle with an insurance policy the firm underwrote on a large wheat farm in Kansas that failed. "What can we learn from the past? Spread out your risk." He gave the entire spiel in twenty minutes and received a round of applause at its conclusion, a first.

Niels had the evening free before departing in the morning for San Antonio. He walked from his hotel to a waterfront restaurant. Inside the cedar structure, fishing nets hung from wood beams, and a bar shaped like a ship's hull gave it a beachy motif.

There was a smattering of people in their thirties and forties at the bar, mostly men, a few couples, and no single women, but he felt an immediate level of comfort and would give it time.

Niels took a corner seat at the bar that provided a full sweep of the room for observing. He opened his wallet and checked his money. He had more than seven hundred dollars on him. He liked the security of cash as a backup when he was traveling in case there was a problem with his credit card. He ordered a Black and Tan. He didn't feel guilty about it because of his morning exercise and the fact that he had a light breakfast and vinaigrette salad for lunch. He was hungry but would hold off for a bit, not wanting to lose the edge of another, stronger hunger that combined with a sense of well-being that all things were possible tonight.

To his rear was a deck that overlooked the bay, which was resplendent in the amber and purple hues of sunset. Niels walked out to the railing for a better view. A great orange sun tottered on the horizon. Along the shoreline recreational boats were docked in a marina.

"This is my favorite view in Tampa."

Niels looked over his shoulder. A woman was standing behind him, dressed in a tee shirt, shorts, and sandals, a tall and colorful drink in her hand.

"It's very beautiful," Niels said as he looked her over. She was in her early forties. She had a native's tan, wide-set hazel eyes, and shapely legs. She was a tad on the heavy side with a body that gave the impression of power in reserve, as if she was more than capable of a rough-and-tumble. That said, there were still curves in the right places and ample and appealing breasts.

She came up to the railing and sipped her drink from a long straw. Niels looked at her and smiled. "Oops," he said, "I forgot my drink." He raised his finger to indicate he would be right back.

When he returned with a Black and Tan in hand, she was right where he left her—a good sign.

She raised her chin to his drink. "This is one of the few places in Tampa where you can get a Guinness and Bass."

Niels turned and faced her. "Well, looks like I was very fortunate to have come here."

She raised her brow with a look that said, "Maybe." Niels let silence fall between them for a beat before he offered to buy her a drink.

She looked at her nearly empty glass and smiled, revealing a missing canine, which gave her a backwoods look. "That'd be great. Let's sit out here." Niels noted a slight twang in her voice that he sensed she was trying to suppress.

At a small round table in a corner of the deck, Niels said, "Allow me to introduce myself. Niels Pettigrew here."

A look came over her as if she approved of the type man she was sharing a table with, but mingled in with that look, there was a fixed slant to her gaze that indicated a difficult life of living paycheck to paycheck. "Bobbie Jo Caulfield," she said as she subconsciously rubbed a ring where a wedding band would go. It was an inexpensive copper band with a cheap green stone in the middle.

"You're not from here, are you?"

"Philadelphia."

"I thought you were a big-city guy," she said. "What brings you to Tampa?"

"Business trip." Niels shrugged his shoulders and made a face to indicate enough said. He took a long swallow of his Black and Tan.

Bobbie Jo took a sip of her drink and nodded her head as though to say, "No problem." She looked out to the bay as the top of the sun sank below the horizon, all the while fidgeting with her ring.

Divorced, Niels thought. *She probably feels failure from it.* "Are you local?"

"I'm originally from Arkansas. Been here for going on twenty years." Her tone said, "It hasn't been easy."

Niels's mind was working out how to get her from here to his hotel, not discussing the difficulties of her life. "I see." But if she wanted to open up, he would listen.

And listen he did. By her third drink, Bobbie Jo's accent thickened, bringing to mind molasses flowing down the Ozarks. She told Niels her life story, from getting married at eighteen in Arkansas, moving to Tampa, where her abusive husband worked on a fishing trawler, getting pregnant at twenty, divorcing at twenty-two, and then scrambling through an assortment of odd jobs before finding employment as a tour guide on a sightseeing boat. "My best job." She shrugged with a "woe is me" expression.

Feeling obligated to not yet abandon the conversation at hand, Niels asked about her child.

"He's serving seven to ten for grand theft auto." Bobbie Jo shook her head and looked away. "My life would make a good country western song." She looked at Niels, and in her eyes he saw that a tacit understanding had been reached that they were from different classes, different worlds.

Niels had trouble listening to her prattle on about her favorite celebrities. She seemed to have total recall of every movie they had ever been in … or some reality TV show that he knew nothing about. But at the same time, he found her a fascinating subject.

"May I be so bold as to suggest to you, Bobbie Jo, that we go back to my place."

A glimmer of hurt flickered in her eyes, a look that said, "Do you think I'm that easy?"

Niels was upset with his impatience. This woman was poor, and this was an opportunity for her that didn't come along very often. *Spend some time and money on her and you will be rewarded in the end.* "How about we go inside and I buy you dinner and we go from there?" Niels said.

Her twist of uncertainty vanished. "I would like that." A wide, country-girl smile split her face, but even that couldn't erase her air of hardness that seemed ingrained.

Niels had sea bass, and Bobbie Jo had a steak. Both were excellent, and Bobbie Jo had lemon meringue pie for dessert. She left nothing on her plates other than a T-bone and potato skin.

"I would like to have a latte outside on the deck." She looked across the table, her gaze that of a negotiator.

Niels felt as if he was buying sex, not that he minded. "Of course."

Niels's hotel room had a king-size bed, and he anticipated they would use all of it. Once inside she pulled Niels's polo shirt out from his trousers and lifted it up, but she stopped at his shoulders. "Whoa, nice body," she said as Niels completed the removal. She reached up and tousled his ever-growing thicket atop his head. "And nice hair too." She slipped out of her tee shirt and adeptly undid her bra. Her breasts were all that he had imagined. She dropped her shorts and underwear, and to Niels's surprise, there was a green tattoo of a lizard below her belly button with an extended blue tongue above a wiry sprout of pubic hairs. Niels felt a twitch of uncertainty. If she could put a tattoo there, what else could she do? But his avarice sexual desire vanquished the thought as he told himself she would probably do just about anything he wanted in bed.

After Niels completed undressing, Bobbie Jo's mouth hung open as she admired Niels's member. "God Almighty," she hooted, "that's one helluva of a stump-daddy you got there." She shoved Niels playfully toward the bed. "Me and Lenny wanted to fuck you the moment I saw those big shoulders out on the deck."

"Lenny?"

She pointed to the lizard on her stomach. "Lenny the lizard. He's what you call my voyager."

Niels wanted to ask if she meant *voyeur. Say nothing*, he told himself as he turned to the bed and pulled back the covers.

"Lie on your back, big boy," Bobbie Jo said as she swept her hand toward the bed, "and spread your legs good and wide."

Without hesitating, Niels obeyed.

"First thing I need to do is to head on down south of the border and lick you inside and out like a hungry dog," she said through a crooked smile.

Oh my, Niels thought, *what have we here?*

She got on the end of the bed and faced Niels. "I got to get you good and lathered up," she said as she straddled her legs inside his and burrowed her head over his crotch and began licking from the base up to the head.

After several long and excruciatingly delightful licks, she raised her head and took in Niels with a look that could only be described as redneck severe—the nose scrunched, the lips parted like a snarling dog. "Don't you go shootin' your load early," she said, "or Lenny will get upset."

Even in full pant, this set off alarms in Niels. She definitely was not all there, but was she dangerous? He would have no problem overpowering her, or so he thought. But his libido told him, *It's fine, just fine. Get on with it.*

On top she really got into it with loud grunts of pleasure, "Ahh … Ahhh, ohh … ohh." She was yelling, "Yee haw!" while twirling her hand in the air as she rode him like she was riding a bronco. She called it cowgirl.

The second time was missionary style, and she had been strong down the middle, her legs wrapped around him like a vise, thrusting and grinding with abandon.

She had given Niels her cell number and told him to call next time he was in town. "You fuck as good as you look … and with a big old stump-daddy to boot."

Niels wasn't the least taken back by Bobbie Jo's crudeness, though Lenny the lizard and that general hardness about her had given him pause; however, her unpredictability had also quenched something deep in his core that he hadn't felt since Spain, a complete and utter sense of carnal satisfaction.

And though he found her talk mindless, she made great material for the journal. He felt more than compensated, and he liked the idea of having a woman, even one a bit crazy with a lizard tattoo that she spoke of in the third person, with no strings attached awaiting his call.

As a matter of fact, Niels may just need to return to Tampa in two weeks for some follow-up work on his presentation. He couldn't wait.

After a couple of uneventful days in San Antonio and Portland, Niels returned to work and immediately scheduled another trip to Tampa. It was more than the sex. There was something about Bobbie Jo that attracted him. He wrote in his journal,

> Bobbie Jo is an uneducated, backwoods woman who lives paycheck to paycheck and takes life on as it comes to her. And with it comes an edge to her that draws me. It seems that sex alone is not enough. There's a down-and-dirty physicality about her that piques the predatory slumdog in me that pushes an entirely new set of buttons that I enjoy turning on. This is a wide chasm from whom I used

to be, but I don't dwell on that. And as Nina would say, I look forward, always forward.

* * *

Mary had a situation at work and had canceled their Wednesday tryst at the last moment, and so by the time Niels returned to Tampa, the slumdog in him was barking loud.

After he left the Tampa office, where Niels went over the same material but with a different allegory about shipbuilders in fifteenth-century Spain, he headed for the same restaurant on the water where he first met Bobbie Jo.

He ordered a Black and Tan at the bar and went to the empty outdoor patio. The sky was overcast, and there was a chill in the air.

"There he is."

Niels turned from the railing and saw Bobbie Jo approaching. She was in slacks and a white shirt with a name tag over the pocket that read, "Henderson's Cruises." Slung over her shoulder was a canvas satchel.

She came up to him and placed her hand around his neck and kissed him hard, her tongue lashing into his mouth. "I missed you," she said as she reached down and grabbed his crotch.

Niels didn't even bother to see if anyone was looking. He was in full slumdog mode. "Would you like a drink?"

"Later. I lost my job today." She leaned into Niels, her breasts firm on his chest, her face in his. "Let's go to your place. Then you can take me somewhere nice, and I can forget I ever took that dead-end job."

In Niels's room they quickly undressed, and Bobbie Jo told Niels to lie on his back. "I got a surprise for you," she said. "Spread your legs and close your eyes."

"Okay," Niels said as he pretended to close his eyes. He knew she might be dangerous, but what could she do? They were both naked.

She placed her canvas bag on the end of the bed and removed a jar of lotion and began rubbing it on his groin area. Oh, did that feel good. His slumdog was howling over the hills.

"Another surprise," Bobbie Jo said. "Close your eyes for real this time."

"You got me," Niels said. He was in the moment and closed his eyes, wondering what delightful sensation was next. He felt her hand grab his throbbing erection, and then he felt something cold and sharp on the base of his penis.

Bobbie Jo stood at the side of the bed, naked as a jaybird, clutching a six-inch stiletto against his now flaccid member. He felt a cold chill run through him as a wave of fear ran from his head to his toes.

"Don't move one inch, or I will cut that big ole stump of yours clean off." There was a cold, calculating tone to her voice that sent another chill through him.

"I won't," Niels said. "What is going on?"

Bobbie Jo stared at Niels. It was a hard look, and her body looked hard, as if a guy-wire had wound through it and pulled tight. Her breasts appeared rock hard, and the nipples were pointy and elongated as though to indicate her body was on full alert. "You're getting robbed. I saw that big wad of cash you carried last time we had dinner. Best you'd better still have it."

All the air seemed to have left the room, and Niels felt a wheezing sensation in his chest as if he might faint. A thought whisked in his mind that this would be great material to write about … if he lived.

"Okay, I'll do what you ask."

She kept the knife firm on his now deflated member, and with her other hand, she removed two handcuffs from the bag. She put them on his chest and said, "I'm going to tie you up just like Rachel McAdams did to Vince Vaughn." A look of mock surprise came over her face. "Oh, you probably didn't see *Wedding Crashers.* You probably think you're too good for it." She grabbed his balls and squeezed, causing Niels to gasp. "Stretch out your right hand to the bedpost and handcuff it with your left. Careful now."

Niels stretched his right hand out to the post, but his left wouldn't quite reach.

"Scrunch yourself up a little," she said. "And so help me I'll cut you bad if you try anything."

"I'm going to lift my elbow and then move back," Niels said with a question in his eyes.

"Very careful, biggin'."

Niels did so and locked his wrist to the post.

"Now we're almost there." Bobbie Jo dragged the knife tip lightly along Niels's torso up to his chest as she moved forward, the blade firm across his throat. "You think I'm white trash, don't you?" Her tone had an edgy, maniacal tremor to it that shot waves of fear like tiny pinpricks running down his arms.

He thought she might slit his throat. His mind was a swirl of jangled thoughts. "I, ah—"

"Shut up," she said in a furious voice. "Wouldn't take much more to bleed you out like a stuck pig." She placed the knife under his chin and forced his head back so that he was facing the ceiling. "Shut your eyes tight and don't move." Niels did as he was ordered. He felt the knife drag lightly down to his scrotum. The next thing he knew the knife was off his body, and his other wrist was secured to the bedpost.

"All righty then," Bobbie Jo cooed in a creepy voice. She removed a spool of duct tape from the bag, and Niels thought he might soil himself. My God, he was afraid. But he had to stay calm. She stared hard at Niels. Her eyes had a bone-chilling glare.

"What are you doing?" Niels heard the tight pleat of desperation in his voice.

"Shut up, big dick. Big man with your money. Thought you were doing me a special favor with your cheap dinner and fuck."

She tore off a strip of tape and secured it over Niels's mouth.

"Now here's the question." She put the tip of the knife on Niels's scrotum. "After I take all your money." She smiled sincerely like an actress in a play. "Should I cut off stump-daddy and take him home to Arkansas and put him in a mason jar of formaldehyde." She smiled again, this time with a mocking sneer. "Ha," she hooted. "Scared you, didn't I?"

Indeed, she did.

She then went to Niels's trousers and removed six hundred from his wallet. "This will do me just fine." She waved the wad of bills at Niels. "You don't even think about coming for me. I got brothers up in them hills bigger than you and a helluva lot meaner." She laughed and shook her head. Then her tone turned back to scary cold. "I'll tell 'em about that big thang you got, and they will cut it off and roast it over an open fire." With that, she put the knife and tape in her bag, dressed quickly, and left.

> After a maid found NP the following morning, hotel security was called. He convinced them not to call the police, that it was just a prank gone bad. Embarrassed to his core, NP could only imagine what talking with detectives would be like. "So let me get this straight, Mr. Pettigrew. You met this grifter woman for some sort of sadomasochistic sex?"
>
> He wanted out of Tampa ASAP. With towel covering NP's private parts, a maintenance man cut off the cuffs with bolt cutters.
>
> NP dressed and left for the airport. The flight back home offered time to reflect on his experience. Bobbie Jo had frightened the life out of him, and at the same time, it revealed who the real predatory slumdog was. He was a fool, and she was a shrewd grifter who had seen him for what he was—fat-cat philander who had thought her a slum

romp. He had learned his lesson. It came to him in a shuddering whoosh that he really didn't know the first thing about women. In business he had dealt with men and had an innate understanding of leverage and positions of power. But his horndog ego led him into unexpected predicaments, and this last one could have been deadly. From here on out, he promised himself to be more careful, much more careful.

Chapter 11

During the next couple of months, Niels continued his morning exercise routine and got his weight down to 210 pounds. His body was firm and lean, his face an older version of high school. He was once again a very handsome guy.

He continued to have Wednesdays with Mary, and though it was a routine, the sex was still gratifying. And the fact that she was a married woman added an edge of excitement to it. He even went birding with her and John in a group. It was no problem. Mary played it cool, and no one was the wiser.

And through his writing in *Memoir Musing*, which he designated with a fictional character name Neal Pendry, whom he designated NP, he gained a new perspective on himself and the people in his life. He surprised himself at times when something unexpected popped in his head and he typed it into his computer.

> It seems the straitlaced NP who had sex with only one woman his entire life prior to the passing of his wife has transformed into the polar opposite of the man who admired John Muir and all that he stood for. The only remnant that remained from his old self is birding. It seems as though a bawdy

doppelganger had taken control of his personal life much in the manner his wife had done.

The incident in Tampa has made NP gun-shy about hanging out in strange bars, but at a conference in a four-star hotel in Chicago, he met a married sales rep for a computer software company. They had a couple of drinks at the bar, and Niels felt completely comfortable with her. They spent the night in his room. She departed early in the a.m., never to be seen again. No problem, and a much more suitable departure than the last time a woman left his room.

He felt back in his philandering groove, and the incident in Tampa was in his rearview mirror. But a nebulous thought still drifted into his mind on occasion. It felt like he needed something more. He thought back to his time in Spain and that sense of exhilaration that had been vacant from his life.

At work, Niels grew more restless and delegated additional responsibility to Edward and others. His passions were exercise, birding, writing in his journal at night, and of course, sex. Each night he thought out a beginning, middle, and end to the journal. Sometimes he had to fabricate events, but no matter what, it was his story. Where this new desire to write came from, he wasn't sure. But it was there, and he enjoyed the process.

On a Wednesday in December, Mary arrived as usual right on time at four. "After," she said as she looked up the steps, "I would like to talk with you."

"Okay." Niels sensed a turning point.

It had been three weeks since their last time together, and both were ravenous. Afterward, they went into the kitchen, and over tea Mary said, "I want more."

Niels poured a cup for Mary from a blue porcelain teapot with etchings of robins he had bought Laura years ago. "More?"

Mary shook her head and looked off for a moment. "I am falling in love with you, Niels."

Niels had no idea. Their get-togethers were almost like a business arrangement. They would talk some but about nothing of consequence. Idle chatter, he called it, and it was limited at that. Niels poured tea into his cup and placed the teapot on a stone trivet. "What are you suggesting?"

"What if I left John and moved in with you?"

"Mary, I am very fond of you." He reached for the half-and-half, poured a splash in his tea, and offered it to Mary.

She declined with a shake of the head. "There's a *but* coming."

"Mary, I lost my wife this year. I am not ready."

Mary took a sip of tea and very carefully placed it back on the saucer. She looked up, and in her eyes Niels saw what was coming next.

"I won't be coming back." With that she stood and headed for the door.

Niels let her go. Even if he did talk her back, it would not be the same. What had just transpired would linger over them like a dark cloud.

> NP began the day with a protein shake at five in the a.m. and headed out for the fitness center. He was the first to arrive—he was always first—and it gave him a sense that he was ahead of the competition. In the middle of a vigorous routine on the curl machine, he noticed an attractive woman doing stretching exercises on a mat. He had seen her before, but he had yet to say anything to her other than hello. But today he would make his move.
>
> She had a well-constructed, voluptuous body wrapped in a sheath of honey-gold skin. A thicket of

dark-brown hair curled at her shoulders, framing a finely formed face, a sexy face with high cheekbones that brought to mind the Mediterranean. There was an older, wiser aura about her, as if she had seen many things beyond her years. The woman came over to the leg press next to NP.

"Good morning to you," NP said with chirp in his voice.

Niels mixed fact with fiction for the rest of the story. He did get a few words out of her and figured she was Greek from her inflection and tonal quality. *I am gööd.*

She was receptive in a reserved way, but he did not secure her phone number or call her later in the day and arrange a date for the weekend as he claimed in his journal. He wrote a perfunctory paragraph about work and then hammered away on the computer a true account about his last time with Mary.

The log for the day ended as follows: "Mary exits, and a beautiful Greek woman enters the life of Neal Pendry."

Chapter 12

The office Christmas party was an event that Niels had always snuck out of early in the past. Last year he had finished up his Christmas shopping for Laura and Andrea. This year he would spend Christmas alone, as Andrea was remaining in Australia. She had met a young man and was spending the holidays with his family. He wondered if she would ever spend another Christmas at home. He could not deny the fact that he was looking forward to spending time with his daughter. But he would make do. She had her own life after all.

The party was held in the conference/entertainment room with catered food and alcohol. The women enjoyed decorating with the same decor every year—white and red poinsettias, red and green crepe streamers hanging across the walls and ceiling, pine tree branches sprayed with gold paint, and spray glitter standing in clear glass vases decorated with red ball ornaments.

All this seemed to encourage staff members to let their hair down. There had been some pretty wild scenes in the past, though Niels only knew this from office gossip since he had always departed early. One year a young female staffer started doing a striptease atop a table until some older women whisked her away.

Niels's boss, Patrick Harrington, was a two-fisted Irishman who enjoyed his whiskey straight up and thought it just fine for the employees to let loose once a year. Niels had always worried about lawsuits, and he had suggested no alcohol. But Harrington, who was a reasonable man in every other way when it came to business, would hear none of it. Niels had always been incredulous that Harrington would take such a risk in this day and age. Now he considered it just fine and dandy. He laughed to himself at what an old stick-in-the-mud he used to be.

This year will be different, Niels thought as he looked out his office window, Broad Street covered in a thin coating of snow, Christmas lights dominating the building fronts, and people bustling along with packages held tight against their winter coats, their collars turned up. This time around he was looking forward to the party, for he sensed it would be his last.

Niels waited until the festivities were in full swing until he made an appearance, the time he usually departed. The conference room was long and wide and brought to mind a ballroom. "Jingle Bell Rock" was playing in the background, and the space buzzed with the hum of social conversation and laughter. For the first time, Niels felt in good spirits standing in this room, no longer feeling uncomfortable in the presence of imbibers. Heck, he was one now and then some.

Niels waited in line at the bar for a drink. In front of him was a woman from underwriting whom he couldn't recall the name of. She was wearing a skirt and blouse, and her hair was clasped in the back by a green barrette in the shape of a Christmas tree.

"I like the holiday touch you're wearing," Niels said as he touched the barrette.

The woman turned around, and her eyes widened with astonishment at the sight of Niels. "Oh, Mr. Pettigrew," she said, her expression beaming with the intake of Christmas spirit … and spirits. "This is my favorite time of year."

She was fairly tall, with wavy-brown hair and a friendly, warm face—an attractive face despite the splotches of freckles under her eyes. She had a shapely figure, and her breasts gave an enticing shape to her blouse that sent a surge through Niels. "Yes, Loretta, isn't it?"

She squinted a smile at Niels. "Loretta Sullivan from—"

"Underwriting," Niels cut in. "You folks have done a bang-up job this year."

They moved to the bar, standing side by side. "What are you drinking, Loretta?" Niels said as he held the bartender's gaze with his. She told him whiskey sour. He ordered two and turned to her. "Has anyone told you lately that you are one fine-looking woman?"

* * *

Patrick Harrington's office was on the top floor and had a sweeping view of downtown Philadelphia. It was Monday morning, and Niels faced an imposing mahogany desk behind which sat a flummoxed executive. In the distance was the faint ringing of a bell coming from the direction of Independence Hall. Harrington was a bull of a man with a thrash of steel-gray hair like iron filings. He sat back, his chin atop folded hands, his face one large grimace. "Niels, what the hell were you and that woman thinking?"

Niels thought back to last Friday and the office Christmas party. After four whiskey sours and two margaritas, he and Loretta went to his office and engaged in unbridled, get-down-and-dirty sex atop his desk. In the wee hours, the cleaning crew had discovered their lifeless bodies—Niels buck naked and draped over his desk, Loretta in her panties and out cold on the floor—and they immediately called security. "It was my entire fault, not hers." A wave of relief came over Niels as he said, "I'll make it easy for you, Patrick." He nodded as if he was mustering the wherewithal to continue. "I'll hand in my resignation, but please let the woman, Loretta Sullivan, keep her job."

"She will be let go today."

"You need to stop that now." Niels leaned forward, his eyes steady on his boss's. "We've all made our mistakes, have we not, Patrick?"

"What are you implying?"

"That you have had your dalliances with female staff members in the past."

A vein began pulsing in the suddenly red neck of Harrington. "Are you blackmailing me?"

"Yes, that's exactly what I am doing."

"She can't stay here."

"Transfer her."

Harrington picked up his phone. "Get me underwriting." After he saved Loretta from the firing squad, Harrington stood and straightened the knot of his red tie, which stood out boldly against his crisp white shirt and blue suit. "Happy?"

"Yes." Niels stood.

"You have twenty minutes to clear out your desk. Security will escort you from the building."

* * *

Christmas was a quiet time at home. Niels never got around to hanging any of the Christmas decorations that Laura had always taken care of. He did buy a Douglas fir, but he didn't put it up. He Skyped Andrea from his laptop. Her grainy image on the screen sent a wave of melancholy though Niels. "Hello, Dad. There's someone here I want you to meet."

A young man came onto the computer screen. "Ian Donley here." He had a thicket of dark curly hair that framed a lean face, a likable, smiling face.

"Hello, Ian, nice to make your acquaintance."

After a bit more chitchat, Andrea came back on the screen. She squinted into the screen. "Oh, Dad, even with this hazy reception, you look so young and handsome, and you have let your hair grow out."

Niels had to remind himself that until recently he had been an overweight teetotaler. It seemed another lifetime ago.

"Yes, I have made a few changes. For one I have resigned from work."

"Really?"

"I want to devote my time to birding and writing."

"Writing what?" Andrea asked.

"It's sort of a fictional memoir, you might say."

"Well," Andrea said in a curious tone. Even on the twelve-inch computer screen, Niels saw a haze of concern in his daughter's eyes. It wasn't as if she was seriously worried, but it was more a look that asked, "Who is this man?"

After he hung up, a pang of loneliness gripped Niels. Christmas felt empty without a wife and daughter in the house putting up a Christmas village and colorful decorations, a nativity scene under the tree, the aroma of sugar cookies baking in the oven, and Bing Crosby Christmas songs in the background. It seemed as though that wave of tension that was always present in Laura's house turned down during the holidays.

But as soon as the new year rolled in, she was back to her old self. "I got a call from Reverend Pritchard." The arms would fold across the chest, and Niels would get the look. "You never completed the assessment report for the church's addition. I don't care what is going on at your work." And so it went. Christmas seemed light-years in the past, as did any thought that he had ever enjoyed being in his wife's presence.

After the holidays Niels ratcheted up his workout routine, spending more time at the fitness center. The beautiful Greek woman had not been around, and just when he was giving up hope, she reappeared.

"Haven't seen you lately," Niels said as she stretched out on a mat. Her olive skin had a deeper hue, her hair a sunny glow. Her body was like a lovely fruit in need of plucking. She was ravishing.

She had one leg crossed over the other, head turned over her shoulder, the top of her leotard stretching tight against her torso. She looked at Niels and smiled her intriguing smile.

Niels began his routine, going from one piece of equipment to the next, checking on her from the corner of his eye. She sat on a bench at the pull-down lat equipment next to Niels, who was grinding away on a sit-up machine. "We work hard," she said.

Niels stopped in the forward position, his chest against the cylindrical pad. "Yes, we do." He waited until she finished a set and went behind her. "It is better to pull down in front of your chest and not behind your neck."

She turned and looked at him, her eyes saying, "Go on."

Think bold, Niels told himself. He placed his fingers below her neck. "You can aggravate your spinal column." He grabbed the bar with both hands and brought it down in front of her and up. "Like this."

She placed her hands next to Niels's, and together they pulled down. He let go, and she continued up and down. "Keep your back straight." Niels placed the heel of his hand in the middle of her back. Her body was firm, and he had the strongest desire to wrap his arms around her and bury his head into her neck.

"It is good," she said as she finished her set. "Thank you." Her eyes took in the measure of him. What eyes! They were velvety brown and knowing, as if she understood him completely.

Niels stepped over to her side and said to her, "I would like to ask—"

She raised her hand for Niels to stop. "I must go." She got up and walked out the door, not looking back.

Chapter 13

By late winter Niels's manuscript had swelled to 250 pages. In the story a rousing affair with the Greek woman was in full swing, but in reality he had made little headway.

His advances were adeptly brushed aside with an enigmatic smile or a look as if she was considering before she turned back to her exercise routine. He had introduced himself, "Niels Pettigrew here," but she had only bowed her head in acknowledgment and moved on to another station. She was never rude, and she didn't tell him to stop bothering her. No, there was always a glimmer of interest toward Niels as if there still may be hope.

He decided to stop playing it coy. He would ask her directly if she would go out with him, even if he had to follow her out the door. Playing it coy with this woman was not an option. And all the while her seemingly partial interest made her all the more desirable. My God, he wanted her. He fantasized about lying naked on a Mediterranean beach with her, her body warm and erupting with the passion he knew she possessed. He imagined what she looked like naked—a sprouty bush of hair covering her vaginal area, full, firm breasts with dark mysterious nipples. But she had not been at the gym for almost two weeks now, and he promised himself that if she returned, he would do everything in his power to win her over.

In the meantime, he had hit a dry spell. Without his business trips, there was little opportunity for romance. He continued to go birding with his group, but he had already tapped that one dry. He had considered going against his instincts and going out to local bars again, but after his incident at Mickey's Taproom and with Bobbie Jo, he could not pull the trigger. And besides, all the local ones appealed to a younger crowd, a situation he wasn't comfortable in.

His entries in his memoir were now completely fictional, but he enjoyed the process of storytelling. His schedule was morning exercise and then writing until lunch. He would take a two-hour break of running errands and then go back to writing for another two hours in the afternoon. At the library, he checked out books on the craft of fiction writing and began reading authors such as Fitzgerald, Hemingway, and D. H. Lawrence. He could not put down *Lady Chatterley's Lover.* He studied how these brilliant storytellers constructed their masterpieces, getting from one point to another in a seamless manner. He admired how they strung words together to form something so utterly beautiful and compelling.

Niels had read *For Whom the Bell Tolls* in college, but after he reread it, he was captivated by Hemingway's ability to use simple words to evoke such power. He had learned through his studies that the title was based on a passage from a poem by John Donne titled "No Man Is an Island."

> No man is an island entire of itself; every man
> is a piece of the continent, a part of the main;
> if a clod be washed away by the sea, Europe
> is the less, as well as if a promontory were, as
> well as a manor of thy friends or of thine
> own were; any man's death diminishes me,
> because I am involved in mankind.
> And therefore never send to know for whom
> the bell tolls; it tolls for thee.

He thought of the peal of church bells during his first day in Barcelona and the heightened sense of awareness that had come over him. Was he, Niels Pettigrew, an island to himself, a man out only for his own self-satisfaction, or was he passing through a stage that needed to be passed through with a mix of literature, creative writing, and philandering? Was this jumble of life changes propelling him toward some end game, a new life?

When he read the scene in Hemingway's novel of the rebels' executions outside the village church, it was as though he sensed every nuance of fear. He could smell the sweat on the soldiers about to be shot and feel the aura of death that hung in the air. He even posted a quote by the great man on his desk. "From things that happened and from things as they exist and from all the things you know and all those you cannot know, you make something through your invention that is not a representation but a whole new thing truer than anything true and alive, and you make it alive, and if you make it well enough, you give it immortality. That is why you write and for no other reason that you know of. —Ernest Hemingway."

His story was a lightweight in comparison, but he sensed that there was more to come, more for him to learn as a writer and a man.

He remained vigilant with his writing and workouts during the week, but on weekends Niels took a break and spent his time birding, sometimes by himself and other times with his group. He was amazed how his relationship with Mary had returned to that of birding acquaintances. On occasion he still drove with her and her husband to meet up with their birding group, and the conversation was congenial and friendly. She acted as if their affair had never occurred. This intrigued Niels, not that he had any problem playing his part, but once again he realized how little he understood about women. They didn't think like men.

So how was he going to solve the problem of meeting women? It came to him—kill two birds with one stone. He would join a writing group, preferably with a majority of women.

An ad in the county newspaper led Niels to join a writer's workshop at the local library. Per the advertisement, the instructor was a published novelist, Leia Childs.

Niels arrived early for the first class, and a posted sign stated that Introduction to Fiction would meet in a conference room in the lower level.

Two women and a man were already in the classroom, sitting at a series of long tables arranged into a square. "Hello," Niels said as he took a seat. He was met by a hello back, one stare, and a woman who ignored him because she was immersed in scribbling into a notebook.

Leia Childs's class consisted of three men and nine women—perfect. The group's age ranged anywhere from late twenties to early sixties.

"This is a beginner's class in fiction writing," Leia Childs said as she sat at the head of the class. She asked each individual to introduce themselves. They mostly had white-collar jobs except for one man who was a landscaper. When it was Niels's turn, he stated that he was working on a fictional memoir but mentioned nothing about his former occupation. What was the purpose of it?

"Has anyone brought copies for next week?"

Niels raised his hand. "I have."

"Very good," Leia said. "Now this class will be broken up into a teaching segment and a critique segment." She gave a general review of what she would be teaching—point of view, which she said was "a very simple technique but often misunderstood," story arc, plot, and other basics for writing fiction.

Halfway through, Leia broke the class for a ten-minute break. Niels had already determined which woman he wanted to make his advance on—Leia Childs. He had Goggled her and found out she was originally from Michigan. Each of her three novels took place in a rural part of her home state. Her books had received accolades from various critics. One said, "A compelling story of one woman's fight for independence in the backwoods of the Upper Peninsula."

Leia Childs had reddish-brown hair that she wore in a ponytail. There was something country in her expression, an aw-shucks look that was complemented by an air of intelligence. Though not bad looking, she wasn't what one would call pretty, but rather she was a big-boned woman with a hard-edged body that appeared familiar with manual work. There seemed nothing of excess about her—no excess weight, no excess word—but something in her gaze when she had looked at Niels for a tic too long and when he had volunteered his story offered hope. It was a look of one appraising livestock, a look that said, "This one will do me just fine."

For the remainder of the class, Leia went over the different options in point of view or POV as she called it. "In third person, get inside a character's head and tell the story as she sees it but through the narrator's voice."

Niels had studied POV thoroughly and realized its importance. He had determined that the third person was his choice. He had read excerpts of Leia's novels, and she had used third person in two, but in her first book, she had employed the first person.

Before the class ended, Niels passed out copies of the first thirty pages of his manuscript. "It's a fictional memoir," he told the class. His announcement was met with silence, an appraising silence that said, "We will be the judges of that."

After Leia dismissed the class, everyone departed. It was nine thirty at night, and Niels assumed they all had work in the morning. All made a beeline for the door except for him and his teacher, whom he had discovered on her website spent a semester teaching two classes in a MFA program at a local college while her husband worked back home in Michigan as a mechanic. *Very interesting.*

The second class began with Leia giving instructions for the critique of Niels's story. "The writer cannot speak until the class has finished with comments." She paused, her pale blue eyes narrowing. "Be civil and constructive in your appraisal. Who would like to go first?"

A heavyset woman in her midforties, Mary Lou, blurted out, "I'll do the honors." She was the one who had not acknowledged

Niels before class last week as she wrote furiously in a notebook. She cleared her throat and began. "First off, this fictional *memoir* should be in first person. Second, the protagonist has not one socially redeeming value, and third, I found the woman Nina as disgusting as what's his name." She pursued her lips, her eyes two angry slits. "And I found the constant reference to a large penis so very distasteful."

Another classmate, the landscaper, found the writing style effortless but the subject matter a bit over the top. The critiques broke down by gender—the woman in full attack mode and the men more sparing. One man, an attorney, found it, "A bit far-fetched, but you write in a smooth, easy-to-read style."

That was as good as it got for Niels. Everyone else picked the story apart with a laundry list from gratuitous sex to syntax. But everyone seemed engage as if the story had triggered something. No one was bored. One woman commented, "The loss of the wife seems to have sent a God-fearing man into a morass of sexual depravation." A comment Niels also would have made not that long ago.

Finally Leia addressed the class. "We must learn to separate personal emotions from the craft of writing fiction." She turned to Niels. "You have a keen eye for observation of things on the periphery." She looked over the class, her gleaming eyes saying, "I dare you to challenge me on this." "I found the writing riveting in parts." She tilted her head to the side, lips pursed as though considering. "Although I had no problem with the sex, the scene in the Barcelona hotel with Nina seemed a bit … hard to believe." Leia raised a cautionary finger, turned to Niels, and said, "Whether something is true or not, the writer must make it believable to the reader."

Hah, Niels thought to himself, *she's on to me.*

After Mary Lou handed out her story for next week, Leia dismissed the class. Everyone hurried out, except Niels and Leia, who was erasing the blackboard.

"Do you have time for coffee?" Niels knew he was out of line, but after his reticence at the gym, he was not going to waste any time.

Leia leaned her head in Niels's direction as she continued to erase the board. "How 'bout a beer?"

The Cock Robin was a dark little moody joint off campus where Leia taught. They took a booth seat in a corner. "I like this place," Leia said with elbows propped up, chin on folded hands. "Nobody knows your name or is interested in finding it out." She smiled mostly to herself. "Plus, they have Pabst in the longneck."

A waitress in her fifties with a seen-it-all look came to the table. "Two Blue Ribbons in the long neck," Niels said.

"Okeydokey," the waitress said through a smirk. She tilted her chin toward Niels, "Glass?"

"No, thank you."

The waitress hurried off.

Niels smiled at Leia. "You must be regular."

"I do like my drinking vessel with a longneck."

Niels had the greatest urge to ask her if there was anything else *long* that she liked, but he caught himself. *Don't get too cute*, he told himself. *She doesn't seem the type.*

After they were served, Leia raised her beer. "To the art of fiction and all the bullshit that comes with it."

Niels clinked her glass and laughed. "Amen to that."

"You had them fired up." Leia took a swig and wiped her mouth with the back of her hand. "That's not a bad thing, getting a reaction like that."

"I don't think I bored anyone."

"You got that right." Leia looked up at the sound of the front door opening. A middle-aged couple slipped into the booth behind her. She lowered her voice and said, "So what made you decide to write."

"I got an itch and decided to scratch it."

Leia leaned forward, her eyes shining mischievously at Niels. "I've had an itch ever since I came to Philly."

Leia's place was a loft in a converted warehouse near her campus. It was a Spartan space and reminded Niels of Nina's loft where she painted. But this was her living quarters, a rough-hewn place with a plank floor, exposed beams, and original masonry walls. An antique oak desk faced an arched window with a view of the street below and the campus. A tiny kitchen with a small bar with two stools added a nice touch to the otherwise drab space with a pullout sofa against one wall and minimal furnishings.

Niels ran his hand over the desktop. "This looks like a good place for storytelling."

Leia was in the kitchen. "Beer?"

Niels took a seat on a bar stool. "Join me." He tapped the stool next to him.

Leia placed the beers on the counter and came over and sat. "So, who the hell are you?"

"Why, me?" Niels said facetiously. He ran his hand down her back. "I am the gentleman you have chosen to help you with your itch."

* * *

Leia rolled off Niels and lay on her back. "That's quite a husky you have there." She propped herself up on her elbow and ran her hand up Niels's leg, fondling his scrotum. "Something that special deserves a name," Leia said as she began stroking the base with her fingers. "I think I will call it Priapus."

Niels had an inkling where she was going. "I take it he was a well-endowed fellow."

"You're on to me." Leia shifted herself down the bed and swung her leg over Niels's body so that her knees were straddling Niels's ankles. She bent down and began licking in long sweeps from the base up to the bulging head that felt as though it might erupt. For a moment he thought of crazy Bobbie Jo and how he had ended up tied to the bed and robbed.

"Priapus, was a minor god of fertility who had a huge cock that was always in full erection," Leia said as she looked up at Niels, a wicked grin spread across her face.

"Hmm," Niels said, "well, old Priapus here is very effective in reaching those hard to get to spots."

Leia grabbed Niels with both hands on his biceps and pulled herself up so that her knees were against his. "Nina or whatever her real name is has taught you well."

"You don't miss much, do you?" Niels said.

"Nor do you," Leia said. "It's a good asset for a writer to possess."

"Make you a deal."

Leia ran her fingers gently across Niels chest. "I'm listening."

"Let us leave the past in the past—"

Leia cut in. "And enjoy guilt-free sex."

"Yes, and one more thing."

Leia had begun kissing Niels's chest. She arched her brow, her beady gaze that of a stalking lioness. "Let me guess. Teach you everything I know about writing fiction."

Niels nodded.

"Under one condition."

"Yes."

"When you write this here," she said, waving her hand in a sweep of the room, "you change it enough so that I am not discovered."

"Deal." Niels offered his right hand to her. She shook it firmly and said, "I believe you have the makings of a hell of a story."

Leia gave Niels a list of books to read, many of which he had never heard of. He had been a fan of murder mysteries and current nonfiction. The writers were mostly from the late nineteenth century up to the mid-twentieth. She told him, "Pay attention to how great writers allow the story to tell itself."

"As if I am along for the ride?"

"Exactly," Leia said.

So off Niels went to the library and checked out Somerset Maugham's collection of short stories, Theodore Dreiser's novel *Sister Carrie*, and Edvart Rolvaag's *Giants in the Earth*—all writers he had never heard of or possibly forgotten.

Once a week over beers at Leia's loft, they discussed what Niels had read the previous week. They never talked about the fiction class. The stories for the most part were dreadful. In the class discussion, Niels offered constructive criticism and discovered he had a real knack for breaking down a story and giving sound advice on rewriting. "Your POV is all over the place," he had said to Mary Lou. "Read John Gardner's *The Art of Fiction*." He received a stone-eyed stare for his effort.

Another story was a real-life memoir about a woman's dysfunctional parents. The story was a chaotic series of events with no storyline. The class shredded her story, and Niels noted how her expression sagged in disappointment. When his turn came, he stated, "This story has great potential with characters waiting to be exploited. I suggest you slow everything down and think about a beginning, middle, and end. I have made comments in the margin that I think can help you put some order in your story." Her eyes brightened, and she nodded a thank-you to Niels.

But the real pro at this was, of course, Leia. She waited until everyone had their say and then offered the final words. She wasn't brutal, but she went right to where the problems lay with succinct and keen analysis like an efficient medical examiner during an autopsy.

And she treated Niels's writing the same way. At her place she had told him, "Too many bedroom scenes with the bird-watcher chick. Repetitive bullshit. And what is this about other than some guy with a big dick?" Leia shook her head and scrunched up her face as if something smelled. "Been there, done that in Spain. Give the reader something to keep their attention beside dicks and pussy, not that I don't enjoy those scenes. But you need to get into this character's head and determine why he went from an admirer of John Muir and all that he stood for to living an amoral or immoral life—not that there's anything wrong with that, mind you—and acting the polar opposite of all that he had been. Do that, and you will have something."

She was right, of course, but Niels was not quite ready to get inside his head. No, he would wait. He had an inkling that he needed to let things play out until the time was right, whenever that would be.

After Leia's review of his manuscript, they went on to what Niels had read for the week. He was halfway through *Giants in the Earth*, which was the story of Norwegian settlers in North Dakota that had been translated to English. "Nothing seems to be lost in the translation," he told Leia. "The style reminds me of Hemingway but without all the excess machismo."

Leia's eyes shined at Niels. "Right on. You've got a writer's eye," she said with in a tone of approval. "Now all we have to do is interject discipline in your writing."

After eight weeks the fiction class was completed, and Leia was in the last week of her school term. Soon she would head back to Michigan and her husband.

"Let's have a special last night together," she said to Niels.

"What do you have in mind?"

"Get shitfaced at the Cock and Robin and fuck the hell out of each other one last time."

The bottle of Schlitz was extra cold. Niels and Leia sat in the same corner booth, the ambience perfect with a dark hue of something out of a '40s noir film. Even the characters at the bar talking out of the side of their mouths and dressed in cheap suits seemed from another time.

"Here's to things learned and those remembered," Leia said as they clinked bottles. She reminded Niels of a tomboy, a modern-day female version of Huck Finn. She seemed not to have a whit of guilt about her infidelity. Nor did Niels for being a party to it. In a book she had recommended by D. H. Lawrence titled *Etruscan's Places*, the author described a shepherd as "not deadened by morals, a free spirit who lives his life not under the rules of man but as he saw fit."

Leia was similar in that she did not allow the morality of the day to interfere with her pursuit of happiness. She took what she wanted and left things as they were before she departed, her husband none the wiser. Niels wondered if there wasn't a tacit understanding that while she was away, they both could indulge in their dalliances as long as it wasn't thrown in the other's face.

"Leia, you have been a grand help to me in my writing," Niels said as he glanced over his shoulder at a splinter of loud laughter erupting at the bar.

Leia turned her gaze from the bar. "You've got a real talent for storytelling." She worked her thumb on the corner of the label on her beer with a look of consideration. "All I did was offer a few profane comments." She looked up, her brow raised. "I did that on purpose."

"I bet I know why," Niels said before he took a long, thirsty swallow. "Damn, that beer tastes good."

"Tell me." Leia had a playful twinkle in her eye that Niels had never seen before.

"You need thick skin to be a writer."

"That's right, and that's why I let those nincompoops shred each other in class."

"They weren't all nincompoops," Niels said evenly.

"No, but it only takes one *crazy* like Mary Lou to make it seem so." She raised her bottle for a refill. "One more thing," she said. "If you can't take the heat, get the hell out of writing."

Niels never heard from Leia again. Nor did he expect to. He liked to think they each got something from their *arrangement*. She had her itch satisfied with old Priapus's help, and he a new appreciation of the craft of writing fiction. From Wikipedia, he discovered that this minor god of fertility was cursed with impotence. Niels looked up impotence and found a secondary definition, "Having no voice in the management or control of affairs." Much to think about.

As a parting gift, Leia gave Niels a written overview of his unfinished manuscript. Line one read, "Give this story a title that encompasses what your character is about, and from that, you, the writer, may steer this vessel on the proper course."

What title could Niels give to an account of the exploits of a philanderer? Of course, *The Philanderer.*

> Leslie was a marvelous teacher, fine companion to share a beer or two or three, and a competent bed partner. But from the start it wasn't anything more than an arrangement—two predators using the other for sexual gratification. There wasn't the anticipatory carnality of that first time with Nina. Nothing more than two people passing through each other's life. NP wondered if in ten years or twenty how much of their time together Leslie would remember. And to that point, all his other bed partners. If he met the one-night-stand sales rep in Chicago in ten years, would she even remember his face or just the size of his dick?

Chapter 14

Niels continued with his exercise routine at the fitness center. He still didn't see the Greek woman. He was busy writing or rather mostly rewriting his manuscript in the morning and afternoon, and he was continuing his healthy eating habits. His body was rock hard, and he had never felt better. The only problem was he had hit another dry spell. He had no desire to torture himself with another writing class. He could hear Leia screaming in his ear, "Been there, done that." On his calendar was a wedding next week in Dallas for his wife's niece, the daughter of Laura's sister.

He wrote that evening,

> It crossed NP's mind that if he were attending the wedding with the wife he would have had little fun or pleasure, as she would have made some excuse to leave the reception early when the booze started flowing. Now he was looking forward with anticipation—life's greatest joy. Look forward, always look forward.

Niels's didn't give NP's spouse a name in the story. He referred to her as *the wife*. Why that was, he wasn't sure yet, but he liked the idea of keeping her nameless.

Niels checked in a day early at the hotel where the wedding reception was being held. It was a sleek, modern building with granite and marble trim on the exterior, complemented by replicate murals touted as Frederick Remington's artwork of the Old West. One was of cowboys branding cattle. Niels knew this as John Muir's picturesque California. Somebody had failed to do their homework.

After he settled in his room, Niels went to a fitness center one block away with a complimentary pass from the hotel for a late afternoon workout. After a good hard session in a nearly empty facility, he decided to walk around downtown. He had been to Dallas in the past for business, but it was in-and-out visits to branch offices. He often flew out the same day.

He walked down Main Street, past major retailers and hotels, some of the buildings modern, others restored. Down a narrow street, Niels came to the Historic North End—mostly brick warehouses transformed into shops and restaurants with outdoor patios and umbrellas covering wrought iron tables and chairs, everything neat and shiny. The spotless sidewalks made of brick pavers with green benches every so often and trees with straight trunks and green leaves lined the narrow street. Something about the place seemed artificially sanitized as though they tried too hard to give it an Old West look with modern appeal.

When he came upon a giant green dinosaur—which looked to belong in a Macy's parade—at the west end of the district, he turned around and headed back for his hotel. It lacked the authenticity and old world charm of Barcelona or even Philadelphia for that matter.

Niels ordered room service for dinner. Something had deflated in him as he walked about Dallas. He couldn't put his finger on it, but he had no desire to hang out in a bar. It all seemed too contrived and desperate. Tomorrow would be better as he planned on going birding at White Rock Lake, a thousand acres of parkland in an Audubon Society–designated bird-watching area and wetlands site.

In the morning Niels decided to skip the fitness center, and he ate breakfast at a diner near his hotel. He ordered bacon and eggs with home fries. It tasted so good. It had been months since he had eaten anything other than fruits and grain in the morning.

The park was within walking distance, but Niels decided to take a taxi. He didn't feel like exercising. He felt like birding. White Rock Lake was situated in the middle of the park, surrounded by hiking and biking trails, arboretum, gardens, and an equestrian center. Again Niels felt as if he were in a manufactured environment, all very neat and pretty, but it seemed so sterile and opposite of the rugged woodlands back home or Ebro Delta in Spain.

At the lake's edge, he came to a series of man-made waterfalls. He spotted a black-crowned night heron darting its sharp beak in the water, trying to snag a fish. But it seemed like a zoo. Everything arranged for one's viewing.

He birded through the lake woods and observed a male black-chinned hummingbird putting on an elaborate courtship display. With his black neck and chin and glossy purple throat band, the male flitted about, flashing his iridescent feathers to a female perched on a branch in a cottonwood tree. He was showing off his aerobatic prowess to indicate he was strong and healthy to sire her offspring.

Duly impressed, the female took flight, and the two birds did a small mating dance around each other until they touched briefly—mission accomplished. They flew off, going their separate ways, her to begin a nest and him to continue to attract more females.

The birdwatcher in Niels thought how beautiful and yet so sad. In this species the only time the male and female spent time together was to mate. He saw the parallel to his own life but did not dwell on it, as his attention was drawn to an indigo bunting perched high in a tree.

He continued around the lake woods and came to a marsh. He scanned the water with his binoculars and caught sight of a black heron and a smaller white cattle egret perched together atop two large branches jutting out of the water—a twofer, two birds in one sighting. It struck Niels as an odd juxtaposition. Yes, both birds were from the same genus, but they were so different in color and size. Normally he would be thrilled at such a sight, but it seemed he was going through the motions.

He returned back to his hotel, showered, and got dressed for the rehearsal dinner at a steakhouse. Laura's sister, Carrie, had told Niels to dress casually. "We'll put on the dog for the wedding," she had told him. Carrie was an adaptable woman, a chameleon who was living life like an actress playing a role, a very good actress. She had married a man who had gotten into the oil business and struck it rich. She was now the southern woman with a Texas twang who said, "Howdy," and, "All right then," as if she had been born and bred on the hardscrabble plains of Texas instead of Bryn Mawr.

Laura had told Niels that as a teenager, Carrie was a hell-raiser with a party streak and a hunger for drugs, anything to get her high, the complete opposite of her older sister. She had gotten pregnant her junior year of high school and had gone out of town for an abortion. It was a family secret that few people knew, and Niels doubted her husband had a clue about her youthful past. At forty-eight she was still an attractive woman with a bright and lovely face and a charismatic excitement about her that drew men's attention. She was a controlled flirt, only going far enough to garner attention and then adeptly averting it away.

The spacious private room at the steakhouse was buzzing with anticipation of tomorrow's big event. It was a comfortable yet elegant space in a Western motif with pictures of cowboys and Indians and wrought iron lamps adorning the dark paneled walls separated at one end by double French doors opening to a veranda that overlooked the historic district.

"Uncle Niels, you look *so* different."

"Mandy, dear," Niels said as a young woman in designer jeans and a powder-blue cashmere sweater approached.

She wrapped her arms around Niels and gave him a big Texas squeeze. Oh my, what a tightly wound body she now possessed. Mandy stood back, smiling big. "I almost didn't recognize you."

"You look all grown up."

Mandy shook a playful finger at Niels, her eyes giving him the once-over. "Whatever did you do to yourself?"

"Oh, diet and exercise," he said, laughing. "And contact lens."

"Wow."

Waiters were beginning to serve, and people were going to their tables. "Join me for a drink later, and we'll catch up," Niels said.

"I'll hold you to it." Mandy was the younger sister of the bride, Margo, and she had completed her first year of law school at U of Texas. She was a bridesmaid in the wedding, and she was situated at the head table with the rest of the wedding party. Niels had a table in back with relatives of the groom, all married couples from West Texas. They were a loud, fun-loving group who had made Niels feel right at home. He enjoyed listening to them talk about high school football and local politics.

One fellow, Uncle Jess, was a heavyset, balding character who sprinkled every other sentence with "sons of bitches." "Them there sons of bitches in Washington, DC, best get it together." Or he would talk about the lack of rain on his ranch. "Sons of bitches, if the weather don't change soon, I best sell my cattle and start a cactus farm." His manner was gruff, but at his core he was a good ole boy with a tongue-in-cheek gleam in his eye that let one know not to take him too seriously. Niels registered in his mind that a colorful character like Uncle Jess could be used somewhere down the line in a story, or at the very least part of his character could be used in some capacity.

He found himself more and more observing people and his environment, all the while appraising and storing tidbits here and there. Leia had told him that when she was meeting new people, she was mentally taking notes of characteristics or the smallest things, such as the way someone held a cigarette, imagining how to describe it in as few words as possible. She had told Niels something that he never forgot. "Good writers see things that others miss. Always look left for things on the margin."

When folks at the table inquired about Niels, he said only that he was from Philadelphia and recently retired. "Oh," one woman with wiry hair and a lean, weathered face said, "you're too young to retire."

Niels smiled and nodded. He then asked her about her ranch, and off she went talking about the price of feed, coyotes, which she called "a real nuisance," and the lack of rain. Niels half-listened while he kept a watchful eye on Mandy, a younger, prettier version of her mother. She was at ease as she conversed, smiling and continually brushing away a renegade tuft of golden hair from her forehead. Her smile was a marvelous contrast of a sparkling row of white teeth backdropped by a tanned face with a hint of rose in her cheeks. She would have fit perfectly on some exclusive Caribbean beach in a lounge chair facing the water, men walking by and stealing glances at the beautiful young goddess. She had a look of Southern belle royalty with an insouciant air that Niels imagined had bedeviled many a suitor.

After the dinner some people adjourned to the hotel bar. During dinner Niels had consumed three Lone Star beers, which had gone down very nicely, and he felt the most uplifted since he had arrived in Dallas. He heard Mandy's laugh as calling directly to him, a trilling *ha … ha-ha … ha* that brought to mind a beautiful songbird. He straightened his tie and absentmindedly ran his hand over his hair. For an instant he thought of the black-chinned hummingbird's mating dance before he made his way toward her.

She was on a corner stool at the bar with three males from the wedding party hovering over her, all talking at once in competition for her attention.

"Fellows, why don't you give me a chance to catch with my favorite niece. I believe I promised her a drink," Niels said in a friendly but forceful tone. The men hadn't noticed Niels approach and turned to stare up at him. Once again he employed his newly developed physique and height as a tool over younger men. He just needed to stand straight with square shoulders and level down a look that said, "I am your physical superior. Now run along, boys."

They looked at one another, dumbfounded for an instant, not sure what to do or say before Mandy said, "Yes, Uncle Niels, have a seat next to me." She kicked out the empty stool next to her, which made a screeching sound.

Niels took a seat and turned to the three unsure suitors. "Thanks, fellas," he said as he raised his hand in a gesture of farewell. "I won't keep her too long."

They grabbed their drinks off the bar and shuffled away.

"Thanks, Uncle Niels, for rescuing me," Mandy said as she placed her hand on his thigh. Her face lit up in a radiant smile. That combined with her warm touch sent a jolt of arousal through Niels.

"Please," he said softly, "call me Niels."

"Oh, you don't want to be my uncle anymore?" Her tone had an air of innocence, yet mingled with it, there was a hint of forbidden sex. It was similar to her mother's flirtatious ways. Was he being reeled in only so far to be tossed back out to sea? Or did this girl of twenty-three consider him as nothing more than one more older man to have some fun with? He looked at her for a moment and then raised his hand to the bartender. "I'll have a Lone Star in the bottle, no glass, and the lady will have—" He turned to Mandy and said ever so confidently, "And what would you like to have this evening?"

"I'll have a sloe comfortable screw." She looked at Niels and then the bartender. "Are you familiar with that?"

The bartender was an older foreign-looking man. "No," he said, shaking his head.

"Southern Comfort, sloe gin, and OJ," Mandy said. She nodded at the bartender and then turned to her uncle. "I really enjoy a slow … comfortable … screw."

Niels took her hand and placed it over his bulging swell. She gaped for an instant before she squeezed hard. "Oh, Uncle Niels."

He felt as though he had an angel on his shoulder telling him, "This is morally reprehensible to even think of sleeping with this young girl. Stop it now, and walk away from her." But then the devil on his other shoulder encouraged him on, "Reprehensible my ass. This is sport fucking at its best, old boy. Young, prime pootang."

My God, he knew this was wrong on so many levels, but the stronger part that had taken control of him ever since he had boarded an airplane for Barcelona overwhelmed any idea of walking away. In his mind he flicked the angel off his shoulder and said to Mandy, "My hotel room. Game?"

Mandy looked around the loud bar, people drinking and shouting all in their own little world of clustered groups. "Let's slip out of here when nobody's looking." She leaned her head toward Niels in a confidential manner. "Have the bartender send a bottle of champagne to your room."

Niels canceled the drinks and placed an order. "Champagne, room 431, pronto." He then handed the bartender a hundred-dollar bill. "Mum's the word." He brought his finger to his lips. "Shh." The foreigner's dour expression split into a wide smile. He nodded and brought his finger to his lips. "Shh."

They waited a couple of minutes until an uproar of laughter from the other side of the bar drew attention. They made it out undetected, save one of the young suitors who caught Niels's eye before they exited the bar. It was a look of jealousy and distrust, a look that said, "Mister, you are disgusting."

By the time they arrived at Niels's room, a bellhop was just leaving. He was a small man with dark, thinning hair, burdened by a look of one carrying an abundance of responsibility, possibly a wife and many children living in a small tenement apartment and scrambling to make ends meet. There was something of the gypsy about this man. He had dark circles under his eyes, and he paid not a bit of attention to the difference in age between the man and woman. Niels thought of D. H. Lawrence's story about the shepherd not deadened by morals. No, this man could not afford to pass judgment on anyone in this life, for he was too busy scrambling to make ends meet. The only thing in this man's gaze was a hopeful anticipation of a tip. Niels handed him a twenty and thanked him, and the man scurried off.

Inside the champagne was opened and waiting on ice.

"Have a seat." Niels offered his hand to a sitting area off his bed as he poured the champagne. Mandy sat on a small sofa next to the window with a view of the historic district.

Niels placed the drinks on a coffee table and sat in a lounge chair kitty-corner to Mandy. "What shall we toast to?" Niels said as he handed Mandy her drink.

"Whatever you like, Niels." She clinked his glass and downed her champagne in one swallow. She placed her index finger on her pouty bottom lip, her expression that of a child wanting more of her treat.

Part of Niels was appalled at what his lothario side was doing, but he wasn't about to call this off. *No*, he thought as she placed her glass on the table, stood, and slipped onto his lap, her arms clinging tightly around his neck. She began kissing his cheek. "You're so cute. You're so cute."

Her body was so very firm and so very tight yet slinky like a viperous snake. No longer did he consider her a child but a hot-blooded woman. Any guilt he had vanished as she ran the tip of her tongue along his lips. She leaned back and looked over toward the bed. "Shall we?"

* * *

A boom, boom, boom pounding sound woke Niels. For a moment he didn't know where he was. He rolled over and found the bed empty. The pounding was coming from the door. "Just a minute," Niels hollered as he reached for his glasses on the nightstand. He felt a bit unhinged. Where was Mandy, and who in the devil was— He looked at the luminous clock on the nightstand. It was three o'clock in the morning!

The pounding continued as Niels looked around for something to wear. He went to the bathroom, wrapped a towel around his unclothed body, opened the door, peeked his head out.

"You son of a bitch," Carrie screamed as she burst open the door and began landing haymakers on Niels's chest. He stepped back as she continued her assault, the door closing shut behind. Niels tried to grab her bare shoulders. She was wearing a slinky cocktail dress, but she shrugged him off, hissing like a wildcat.

"Carrie, what is the meaning of this?" Niels said as he struggled to grasp her arms. He brought her in close, and she began kicking his shins with the toe of her high heels. He lifted her off the ground and brought her in tight, her ample cleavage pressed against him. "Stop it. For God's sake, stop." She tried to wriggle free, but he had her. He had lost his towel in the process, and now he was standing buck naked with his irate sister-in-law in his clutches.

"Let go of me, you despicable, lecherous bastard." The fight was leaving her, and Niels noted the strong scent of alcohol on her breath.

"I'll let go if you promise to stop attacking me."

"You cocksucker! You fucked my daughter."

She tried to wriggle free, but she was now gasping for air. She had spent herself. Niels released his grip. "Who told you this?"

"Jared Broderick," she replied as her mouth hung open for an instant at the sight of Niels in his birthday suit.

He reached down for the towel and wrapped himself.

Niels knew it had to be the fellow who had spotted him walking out with Mandy. "I have no idea what you are talking about."

Carrie stood back and pursed her lip in an indignant manner but with a trace of uncertainty in her eyes. "He said he followed you two up to this room," she said and then paused to catch her breath. The crazed rage had left her eyes, leaving an intensity that Niels found more than a bit appealing. She was a damn fine, good-looking woman. She continued, "And he told me she never came out."

"Where is she then?"

"Are you saying Mandy was never in this room?"

"I was talking to her about my lawsuit I had against the airlines in Laura's death."

Carrie brought her hand to her mouth, an *uh-oh* expression on her face.

"I had settled with the airlines, and it never set right with me." Niels cleared the false emotion from his throat. "I could not hear her in the bar and suggested we go to my room to discuss it further." He raised his palms in front of himself. "She told me I had little options at this point but then proceeded to tell me how much she had always loved her Aunt Laura and how upset she—" Niels again cleared his throat and offered his opened hand toward Carrie in a conciliatory manner. "She and your family were about not making the funeral."

Niels sighed so heavily he thought he had overdone it, but Carrie brought her hand to her mouth, a look that said, "What have I done?"

"We then talked about family and lost track of the time." Niels realized the half full bottle of champagne was sitting on the table to his rear and hoped to God Carrie didn't see it. He placed his hands on her shoulders, his face in hers to block her view, and made a calculated guess that she hadn't yet talked with Mandy. He knew her well enough to know she could go flying off the handle before she got all the facts. "If you ask Mandy, she will confirm every word I said."

"I am so sorry," Carrie said as she placed her hand on Niels's cheek. "Sometimes I act before I think."

"That's a quality in you I always found attractive." Niels leaned forward, his lip inches from hers. He held it there, waiting. Then he brought her into him as the towel again fell from his waist.

"Let me freshen up," Carrie said as she turned.

When the bathroom door closed, Niels quickly collected the champagne bottle and glasses and stowed them in a drawer.

As Carrie emerged from the bathroom, he thought of the black heron and the smaller white cattle egret perched together atop the two branches jutting out of the water at White Water Lake—a twofer, two birds in one sighting.

Niels got little sleep since Carrie didn't leave his room until five. He tried to sleep in, but he gave up and began dressing for the fitness center. For the second day in a row, however, he decided against it. Instead he returned to the little diner and had bacon and eggs with all the trimmings.

He returned to his room. He was tired, but there was an edge of excitement as if he had accomplished a great feat. He went to his laptop and began writing the events of the last twenty-four hours. He found it difficult to concentrate as if he had overdosed on caffeine.

He could not wait to get back home to write in detail about what had transpired. But he did manage to jot down a basic description of yesterday's events, including Uncle Jess. When he finished, he said aloud in a low voice, "Sons of bitches." Indeed.

The wedding was interesting in that Mandy and Carrie acted as if nothing out of the ordinary had taken place, but the young suitor Jared shot a few narrow-eyed glares at Niels. He smiled back at him and offered a two-fingered salute off his eyebrow. Carrie's husband looked like he had been run over by a truck, and Niels assumed he had tied one on last night and probably slept through the entire night of his high jinks with the man's wife and daughter. A twofer.

Niels snuck out of the wedding reception early, took a cab to his hotel, and headed to the airport. Nobody would miss him. Mandy and Carrie were probably relieved that he was gone, and he had the strongest, unyielding sense that he would never see either of them again.

Chapter 15

It was good to be home. After he unpacked and sorted through the mail, Niels took a Schlitz in the longneck out of the fridge and went out to the terrace. He ensconced himself in an Adirondack chair under the elm tree, the moonlight casting shadows over the backyard.

He had considered going straight to his study and writing, but he needed to unwind from the fatigue that gnawed at him. He had gotten little sleep the last forty-eight hours, but it seemed a small price to pay for the material he had for his book.

He would have to change the city and the names and faces, but he would write a chapter about Neal Pendry's exploits at a wedding. He had not a clue how to end the story, but his sense of timing told him it was nearing. So after he wrote the Dallas chapter, he would have to figure out an ending with some sort of implications that alter the character in a profound way. He wished he could talk to Leia about his dilemma, but that would not be a good idea. She was back in her world of two-track gravel driveways, chickens pecking about the yard, and a tractor in the barn. He learned all this from her website, which had a picture of her holding a rifle with a backdrop of pine trees. Her expression was that of one at home in her environs. She had an expression that said, "Do not tread."

He knew Leia well enough to know that a phone call from him would be considered out of bounds. A call from a former male student and former bedmate would not be well received. She seemed to Niels to be a women living as two different people in two different worlds—an author and teacher of the craft of fiction writing at an upscale private college in Philadelphia who had no qualms about infidelity and the backwoods alpha female who had a strict code of conduct for rural etiquette. Niels thought she would never stray from her husband back home, for that would come back and blow up in her face.

There was a connection between the way Leia lived her life and how Niels had transformed his. He was such a different person before Laura's death than he was now. He whisked the thought from his mind that he might someday return to some variation of that person—the lover of all things John Muir, one to possibly do volunteer work again and attend Sunday service. No way.

The Wexford Grove nondenominational Christian church had played a big role in Niels and Laura's life. He had held various positions on the board, using his business acumen to help with funding a major construction project, among other things, that Laura had volunteered him for over the years. He never minded helping those less fortunate, but he had suppressed his aggravation at the time spent on projects involving the church by not wanting to rock the boat with Laura, who wrapped her entire persona around that damn church.

Niels had not spoken with Reverend Pritchard and had no plans to. The phone messages started shortly after Niels canceled his counseling sessions with the preacher. The preacher called a few more times but eventually stopped.

All these thoughts of who he used to be were not prominent in the front of Niels's mind. They were more like distant phone calls with bad reception. They were noted in the back recesses, but right now his priority was completing his manuscript.

So he would bide his time and see where life led him in his writing and in other things.

During the twofer, NP was at his predatory best like a wily fox. The sex with both daughter and mother was intense and satisfying. Marne clung her arms and legs around her uncle like grappling hooks, raising and heaving her young, lean body with a nearly reckless abandon as her energy seemed limitless.

Candice was heavier, by no means fat, but she had more of a mature woman's body. Her breasts, which he suckled on with avaricious delight, were full and surprisingly firm.

Afterward, when the double deed had been done, the exhilaration faded, and in its place was a mental no-man's-land. It was his best night philandering, and yet it didn't seem enough. As though a vague part of him, like an empty echo, reverberated in his heart—if he still had one. Then again it was great while it lasted, but where was the enduring connection?

NP thought of a pair of mourning doves that built a nest in a maple tree in the backyard every spring, both with light-gray plumage. The male had bright purple-pink patches on the neck, and the smaller female had a distinctive cluster of black spotting on her wings. They worked together on the nest, the male collecting twigs and the female building.

What really stuck in NP's mind was the song of either one calling the other back to the nest—coo-oo-oo, co-oo-oo. That haunting melody had a reassuring effect, as if things were going to be okay

> once again this spring—the mourning doves were back. This year was the first time they didn't show, and the silence felt profoundly empty.

* * *

Niels arrived at the fitness center at quarter after six in the morning. He had almost not gone, wanting instead to start working on his manuscript, but something—a feeling, a sense—encouraged him to go.

He began his routine on the row bar. He didn't want to do this. He was tired of the monotony of this entire drill of early morning exercise. He had the strongest urge to walk out and drive home. Then *she* came into the room, the Greek woman. A surge like that of an electric charge raised the hair on Niels's arms. He increased the weight on his station and began vigorously pulling down the bar.

The Greek goddess was stretching on a mat. Only two other people were in the room, and they were at the other end on stationary bikes. Niels finished his set and moved on to the rowing equipment next to the mats. "I thought you had left me for good."

In a sitting position with legs extended, the woman paused between turning her torso one way and then the other and raised her perfectly shaped eyebrows coyly. She looked at him for a moment before she returned to stretching.

Niels pulled the row bar toward him, back and forth, back and forth. He was flummoxed by this perplexing woman. From her previous workouts, Niels figured he had more than an hour to come up with a plan. *Let her get into her workout, and then you can be bold.*

Niels tried to ignore her as he made his way to the various stations, but he kept watching her from the corner of his eye.

By seven, there were more than twenty people working out. Most preferred the tiered double row of exercise bikes and StairMasters. Niels had never preferred them. Nor did the Greek.

"We are different, you and me," Niels said to her as she grinded away on a leg-press machine.

She ignored him until she finished her set. "What is it you want from me?" There was a challenging gaze in those beguiling eyes.

Niels got down on his haunches and leaned his head toward her so that their faces nearly touched. "To lie naked with you."

"Why didn't you say so to begin with?"

"Grand, dinner my place with drinks before," Niels said through an emerging smile he could not contain. "I don't know your name."

She brushed away a whisk of hair from her forehead and said, "Elissa."

"Ah, the mystery lady has a name."

Elissa wagged her finger playfully at Niels and said, "I like humor in a man. Now let me finish my work here, and we will talk after."

Elissa told Niels that Friday night at seven would work, but when he asked for her phone number, she demurred. "Tell me your name again and where you live, and I will be there." She liked red wine, "Any type is fine," she said.

Niels went to the gym every day for the rest of the week, but she never showed. He told himself he was going for the exercise, but his heart was not in the regimen. Each day he worked less and left earlier.

By Friday evening he wondered if she would show. The uncertainty of it made her all the more desirable. Her question, "What is it you want of me?" and her reply to his answer, "Why didn't you say so to begin with?" made it difficult for Niels to stay calm. Good Lord, did he crave that curvaceous, golden-skinned bombshell.

By quarter to eight, Niels's mood had sagged. He went out on the terrace with a 2005 bottle of Robert Mondovi cabernet, a very dry year. The yard looked lovely, the grass and hedges trimmed, the pond cleaned, and the terrace power-washed, all done by Niels who had an abundance of energy during the course of the week.

Managing the yard was something new for Niels. Laura had hired people to do all those things, but now that he had retired from work, he decided to take them on. He bought the necessary equipment and enjoyed the process from pushing the power mower to scrubbing his pond clean. His fitness made the work less of a strain and offered a new type of satisfaction from physical exertion.

> NP was surprised at how little he fatigued from spending an entire day working in his yard. His Nautilus-honed muscles were well equipped to handle his backyard chores, and at times he wished it were harder. This was strange since he had become bored with the tedium of exercise at his gym. *Ah,* he thought, *a little variety is good not only for the soul but the body.*

His writing was now two-part. He would rewrite what he had previously written and still keep an account of each day's events and inner feelings of his character. His closing comments on Dallas had surprised him—where was this insight coming from?—about paralleling his string of one-night stands to a monogamous pair of mourning doves. It seemed as though he was having an internal disagreement. At times it felt like he was only a bystander as if other forces were at work. Fate? Destiny?

Whatever was going on, he was determined at this moment in time to have a rousing, plot-turning entry interjected into the story if Elissa showed. If she didn't, what then? *Stay positive*, he told himself as he turned to the creak of the gate and the picket fence opening.

"Hello there," Elissa said. She reminded Niels of some exotic bird out of its element, one that could take flight and never be seen again if not handled properly. She was wearing aviator sunglasses and dressed in a sleeveless top that fit her body like a glove, calf-high khaki jeans, and a pair of canvas boating shoes. She looked like a model for an advertisement for sailboats or the like. Her cheeks were flushed red, suggesting she had been involved in an outdoor activity. She was the most beautiful and desirable woman Niels had ever laid eyes on.

"Come in. Come in," he said as he heard the excitement in his voice.

"Your house and property are beautiful." Elissa took off her sunglasses, placed them on a wrought iron circular table, and took in Niels's backyard. "Ah, you have a pond."

Niels held his tongue. A little voice, the same one that had coached him with Nina, told him to do so.

"You like birds, I see," Elissa said as she looked up at a wren house hanging from a branch in the elm tree overhead. It seemed she was taking inventory of not only the property but the man who owned it.

"I have wine." Niels went to the table and poured two glasses. He handed one to Elissa and offered her a seat.

"Let us sit in your big green chairs." She leaned her head toward a pair of Adirondacks.

"Of course," Niels said as he gestured for her to sit.

Elissa held her wine up to the light, shook its contents slightly, took a sip, and then a swallow. She sat back and kicked off her shoes. "This is nice, very nice."

A thousand things raced through Niels's mind to say to her, but again he held his tongue.

"You have family?" Elissa said.

"A daughter living in Melbourne, Australia. That's it."

A look of understanding came over Elissa as though she understood Niels's situation completely. Something in her smile—a rare and beautiful thing—seemed to say, "It is all right. I am with you." She smiled again but more as comrades sharing a private moment. "I love Melbourne. It is a wonderful place to sail." There was a controlled excitement in her voice that Niels imagined men found hard to forget. It was like the song of a rare bird that only a privileged few ever are allowed to hear.

Niels held his curiosity and said, "My daughter, Andrea, wants me to come and visit her."

"You must go," Elissa said in a tone that indicated the case was closed.

They settled back and began chatting amicably about general topics. Mostly Niels talked, and Elissa listened as he spoke about his interest in birding and travel to Spain; however, he did not mention his writing.

Finally Niels decided to break the ice. "You are Greek?"

"I am," Elissa said as she offered her empty glass for a refill.

Niels refilled both glasses. "You have secrets, Elissa."

"As do you, Niels." That was the first time she had said his name, and she said it with an added twist as though she knew his deepest thoughts.

Niels cooked tuna steaks on the grill. He had prepared a vinaigrette dressing, a salad of Bibb lettuce and tomatoes, and asparagus that he grilled alongside the tuna. They ate at the table on the terrace. They talked about places they had been to, but she never mentioned who accompanied her or why she was there.

Elissa had been to many places, and all were near large bodies of water—many of the islands in the Pacific, Australia, all along the Mediterranean coastline, and the Caribbean.

During dinner Niels opened another bottle of wine, and after they finished their meal, they sat in the Adirondacks side by side, a comfortable silence under the glow of lamplights bordering the terrace. "I must leave in two hours," Elissa said in a matter-of-fact tone.

"Would you like to go inside?"

Elissa took his hand in hers. There was the most delightful warmth generated from her touch. She looked at him, her face glimmering in the flickering shadows and light. How haunting, how alluring. She looked like some beautiful night creature that had landed in his yard, never to be seen again.

They ended up in the guest room, the second woman Niels had taken there. Without prompt, Elissa undressed calmly and confidently. First she pulled off her sleeveless shirt and bra, and then she removed her jeans and purple thong panties, all done as if it were no big deal.

Quickly Niels followed suit. For an instant they stood and looked at each other, her gaze quick and lovely without a trace of discomfort. Elissa's breasts were entities unto themselves, her nipples, large and brown and oh so beautiful. Her body was all curves in all the right places.

"You have a fine body," Elissa said as she came up to Niels. She ran her hand in a circular motion on his chest, inching her way down. She took hold of him. "You big boy," she whispered. "Big boy."

Those were the same words Nina had used—*big boy*. The accent was somewhat different, but something in the way they both said it with their Euro accents had an arousing effect on Niels. *What was it about European women?* Once again, for a moment and only a moment, he thought about how he couldn't wait to write about what was going to happen.

He kissed her, and their bodies entwined. Niels turned, and they fell into bed on their sides. Niels began kissing her neck and then her breasts, which were rock hard with her nipples drawn up. Niels could have spent an eternity there, but he remembered a time limit and lowered himself to her stomach and then to her private area. Elissa withered with delight as Niels's tongue delved deep inside her.

When he entered her, she gasped and gasped again. "Aww, aww," she said as he began to rhythmically enter and retreat, enter and retreat.

After the first time, they caught their breath for a moment. Then Elissa got on top and rode Niels with her back to him. Afterward, she told him he was the first man who had ever completely satisfied her. "The first I can ride like stallion." The reference again brought to mind Nina. In every way these European women were so delightfully erotic.

Then it was over, as Elissa took her clothes into the bathroom. Niels heard the sound of running water from the sink. She emerged completely dressed. "We have good time tonight, no?"

She looked at Niels for a moment before she raised her hand farewell.

"Wait," Niels said. "I won't see you again, will I?"

She shook her head and said, "No." Her eyes met Niels's for a moment, and then she was gone. She walked down the steps and out the front door. From the window Niels watched her get into a black limousine.

Who in the world was this woman? A Greek heiress or possibly a kept woman of some shipping tycoon? He had an image of Elissa—if that was her real name—on a huge yacht docked in the Aegean Sea, sunbathing in a skimpy bikini on the top deck alongside an older man with dark, wrinkled skin and an aura of power and wealth reeking from his pores.

Like a phantom she had appeared in his life and then disappeared for months at a time before she had reappeared. Now she was gone for good. She seemed to have no permanent roots, but this earth was her home.

Niels took a shower and dressed. Then he went to his computer and began writing.

The following morning Niels woke at five thirty, and instead of going to the gym, he went out the front door for a morning walk. He didn't feel like returning there. It was more than the ennui of the process. He wasn't sure why that was. He just had a sense that his time there for the present had run its course. Maybe it was only to meet Elissa and now allow fate to guide him where it may. He felt as if he was a character in a story written by a higher power, and he was only plagiarizing. Did he, as the secondary definition of *impotence* stated, have no voice in the management or control of his affairs? Was he a sexually potent man living an impotent life?

It was June, and the suppressive summer heat had not yet descended. The neighborhood was prime real estate with stately Victorians and Colonials dominating the landscape. Oak, maple, and birch trees were prevalent along the streets and thoughtfully situated on the grounds. It was a wonderful place to walk and think about his story. He wouldn't change a thing about his time with Elissa, not even her name. He never did get her surname, and like some rock star, she would only be called Elissa.

Chapter 16

Niels carefully wrote and rewrote the chapter about his evening with Elissa. He then went over the entire manuscript and deleted the fabricated over-the-top scenes so that the final product was a memoir with little fiction other than the different locales in some instances.

> Tonight with Elissa was a perfect seduction, but NP wondered about who had done the seducing. Was it a mutual affair? The evening was like a dream—the time on the patio talking with a bronze goddess who had a detached coolness about her that was so damn alluring. Then without any games or idle conversation, they adjourned to his bed and engaged in blissful, out-of-this-world sex. Every movement she made, from kneading his back with her supple fingers to rhythmic thrusts that ended in a perfectly synchronized orgasm. My God, it was sublime.
>
> NP watched from the bedroom window as the black limousine drove off, and with it went his most interesting and challenging conquest to date. He felt a chill in the air and closed the window. Then

he yanked the twisted rat's nest of sheets from the bed. He put them in the hamper and got clean linens from the closet in the hallway, but for whom? Another woman to ride off into the night never to be seen again? Once again it was over, and once again the silence felt empty.

The following two weeks, Niels spent carefully proofreading the manuscript, reading it out loud to himself. Even though he hadn't gotten inside the head of his character as Leia had advised, he decided it was a ribald tale of a philanderer, nothing more. He told himself the story was good as written.

With creative writing dominating his life, he had little contact with people other than weekends with birders. Some days he never spoke to another person other than saying hello to neighbors on his morning walk. It didn't bother him, though he did wonder if it wasn't a bit odd. He thought of John Muir going off into the wilderness for months without any human contact to find solace among the great outdoors.

Was it, Niels thought, that he was seeking his solace through his writing and now the challenge of how to get published. Leia had told him that for an unknown author to get published was nearly impossible. His first step should be to find a literary agent, which was still a long shot. He did research online and found that a query letter would include publishing credentials, which he had none of, some variations of a synopsis, and anywhere from the first five pages to sample chapters of a book.

He purchased books on how to get published and found most of it fluff but with a few buried hidden gems, such as how to write a query letter and synopsis. He also bought a two-thousand-page *American Heritage Dictionary* with illustrations and a wooden book stand for his desk. He was beginning to feel like a writer.

Niels painstakingly wrote three synopses—a half-page one, a full-page one, and a two-page synopsis. He started on the longest first and found it difficult to capsulize four hundred pages in such a short space, but after two days of grinding, he finished it and went on to the other two, each one easier than the last. Then he studied sample query letters and noted the humble yet confident tone. He also noted there was not a lot of excess. These letters were bare-bones, succinct gems written by accomplished writers. He spent a week on his query letter, and finally he was satisfied.

A website that listed literary agents offered each genre they represented and how they liked to be queried, and even better, it listed their e-mail address and website.

Niels started at the back of the list, figuring that most people started at *A* and worked their way forward. Many may have given up before they had even reached halfway.

He sent his first query to Zinehurst Literary Agency LLC in New York. Most of the big ones were located there. They requested a query letter and nothing else. If they were interested, they would get back to you. If you hadn't heard anything in four weeks, then you can assume they have passed. This seemed a rather cold way to do business, but it was probably necessary with all the people like his writing classmates sending off their atrocious work.

He decided that he would send the query letter but with the first four pages. What were they going to do? So he e-mailed it off and then moved on to the next in line. He studied each agency website and the authors they represented and tweaked each query that he thought would appeal to the reader. "I noted that you represent Stanley Hooper and thought you might find my novel, *The Philanderer*, a different take on a similar genre."

By the second week of sending out queries, the rejections came, mostly form letters, all with a variation of the following: "Thank you for querying us regarding your manuscript. Unfortunately, after careful consideration, I have decided to pass. I wish you the best of luck in finding representation."

One left Niels blurting out, "Sons of bitches," when it ended with a postscript, "I just didn't love it enough."

By the time Niels reached the Ps, he knew this was a fruitless endeavor. Plus, each rejection letter he received was like a small dagger to the heart. Did they even get as far as reading his synopsis and sample pages? He went online and found professionals who would edit and critique a story. But these people were strangers, and they were expensive.

He took another look at Leia's written critique of the first twenty pages he had submitted to the writing class and was impressed again with how she found *it* "a breath of fresh air and a unique voice. Don't let anyone change that." She had told him over beers one night that the only people she let look at her work were a small cadre of trusted friends who knew what they were talking about.

Niels decided to take a break from it all and spend tomorrow birding in a state park nearby.

For breakfast Niels had a cheese omelet and fried potatoes. He was getting away from fruits and grains in the morning. He thought it okay because he had stopped having beer before dinner. Why? He didn't know other than it didn't seem appealing anymore. He included all of it in his journal, which he still wrote in daily. And why that was since he had finished the story, he wasn't sure of either. He kept telling himself not to overthink these things and that seemed a sensible approach, for dwelling on it was useless. A faint voice in his head whispered on occasion, "Having no voice in the management or control of affairs."

> NP had transferred his philandering zeal and energy into attempting to get his manuscript published, relaxed on his stringent diet, and slackened his exercise routine. He no longer felt like the philanderer but a writer trying to publish a story about one. He did not concern himself with why he had changed so suddenly. Instead, he concentrated on the steep challenge presented by the publishing industry. And after one rejection letter after another

without even a request for materials, he began to have doubts.

Niels packed a lunch and stored it with water and his binoculars in a small backpack and headed off to a local park.

It was midweek, and he found the park empty save a few people who were fishing down past the picnic area at the lake's edge. Surrounding the lake was a thicket of woods with trails maintained by volunteers, including Niels, who had been remiss for some time now.

Birds were audible but hidden in the foliage of the big trees. Occasionally he spotted one changing branches, and they were your garden-variety type of sparrows, crows, and catbirds. He heard the rapid tweet of a house wren and then a *che-che* followed by silence until it repeated the process. Niels's mind flashed back to Laura's funeral, how that little bird's song had affected him that day.

He veered off the trail to a clearing of wildflowers and tall grass. He sat on a stump at the edge of the meadow and removed a sandwich of natural turkey breast on pita bread with bean sprouts. He took a tired bite of his sandwich and chewed the bland food. It was getting a bit mundane eating the same healthy thing every day. He took another bite and returned the partially eaten sandwich to its baggie. He had a craving for a steak and cheese sub he used to treat himself to at a local deli, but he had not taken that step yet. The warm air with rising humidity took his mind off food. He was here to look for birds, after all, so he would sit and look and think about the dilemma of trying to publish his story.

He reached back for the sandwich, took a bite, trying to convince himself how good and healthy it was, and scanned the treetops. Nothing—it was if they had disappeared.

He needed to think outside the box in regard to making his book a reality much like he had done during his career. Crunching numbers and calculating the odds and then calculating some more, Niels looked at all sides of a problem and then from outside looking in. Oftentimes, when he let his mind drift into a vacuous state of nothingness until he saw things from a different perspective, he found success by coming up with an intuitive leap that allowed him to take an entirely new tact that revealed the core of many a problem.

So there had to be an answer that would make literary agents line up to sign him up. Just then the flapping whoosh of a large wingspan broke his thought.

High up in a pine tree was a large dark bird with white markings on its head, breast, and legs. Niels reached for his binoculars. It was huge. Was it an osprey? What was it doing inland? It lived along coastlines and hunted fish. It dug its large hooked claws into the thick branch, anchoring itself like a sentry on duty. The head moved incrementally as if it was calibrated, scanning the surroundings, its sharp yellow eyes seemingly missing nothing. Niels sat perfectly still as he peered through the lens at this magnificent bird of prey. "Chewk-chewk-chewk," it called out before it flapped its wings and flew off.

Niels wondered if it was lost or possibly escaped from a zoo. Or had it adapted to hunting off the park's inland man-made lake that had been stocked with fish? Had this bird thought outside the box and found safety in the shelter of the high trees and plentiful food provided by the lake?

Like that osprey, Niels needed to adapt in finding good hunting for himself in search of an agent. The osprey was living outside its habitat, and Niels must do the same. Birds of prey try not to be detected when they're hunting, but Niels must do the opposite. He must draw attention to the author, Niels Pettigrew. It struck him like a thunderbolt. Start a blog. He knew nothing about it, but how hard could it be? Research it online and go for it.

* * *

Niels found a website that offered instructions and set up his blog. It wasn't easy, but after three days he had it up and running. He decided to call it *Musing from a Philanderer.* In the top corner, he inserted a profile of Giacomo Casanova and under it a quote, "I have delighted in going astray." Ahead of time he wrote a series of posts all pertaining to the art of meeting and seducing women. The bawdier, the better. He started each post with advice. "Never allow a woman to see anything but confidence or disinterest on your face. My first option is the latter." "Exercise and good nutrition are essential." "Never confuse love with sex."

He joined Facebook and set up a fan page titled *The Philanderer.* Men would be most interested in the blog, so on Facebook, he joined a number of groups affiliated with sports. He then posted tidbits about his blog three times a day.

Soon the blog had a following with comments and questions. By the end of the first month, he had three thousand followers. But he needed to make a big splash and obtain publicity. He posted a comment on a radical women's liberation blog, taking a line from Hamlet. "The lady doth protest too much, methinks." He signed it with the signature *fellow human being* with the link to his blog.

Oh my God, did the sparks fly. His blog was lambasted by irate women and a few men who were appalled by his insensitive comment. "Your use of William Shakespeare to tweak your nose at an important subject such as freedom for women is despicable."

The next day Niels posted on the women's blog, "Why don't you girls and feminist boys loosen up a little? I suggest trying cowboy style with the opposite sex … or the same sex if that works for you."

Again his blog was overwhelmed with comments, but this time he received a few in support. He posted all comments on his Facebook page and on the wall of every organization he had joined.

This was hard work. After a long walk at the crack of dawn, Niels went to his computer and began his daily blogging. First he read every comment. Then he wrote out his *Words of Wisdom for the Day*. "There is no such thing as bad sex. The only bad sex is no sex." "Try harder, stay longer." He answered questions, some humorous and others serious, all about meeting and bedding woman. "I'm overweight and have no luck with women. Suggestions?" Niels responded, "Do what I did—exercise vigorously and diet. Make it hurt. Once you have lost the weight, get back to me, and we will set up a plan to make you king of booty!"

His diligence was rewarded in raising his readership to ten thousand. But then he was banned from the feminist blog, all his comments instantly deleted. He protested loud and long on his blog and all over Facebook about the cowardice of those who back down when things didn't go their way.

He wrote for his followers to lodge complaints on the women's blog. In the meantime, Niels contacted a prophylactics company and a porn magazine and asked if they would be interested in advertising. Both agreed, and now he was making money through his writing. Always in the back of his mind was the mission—get his manuscript published.

Then came the break Niels had hoped for. A Los Angeles newspaper wanted an interview about his blog. It was to take place via the Internet, which allowed Niels time to frame his responses. Over the course of three days, he exchanged e-mails with a woman reporter, and he saved every question and response in case anything was twisted out of context.

The reporter had done her homework and inquired if the death of Niels's wife had triggered a change in personality. It surprised him that she would know such a detail since he had never mentioned it on his blog. This woman was thorough. Niels responded that he lived each day to its fullest and let the past stay in the past.

She asked about the loss of his job and his trip to Spain. How in the world did she know that? But she never got any further. By the second day of questioning, Niels decided to see who this woman was and did some research.

Madeline Dowdy had never been married. She was a career journalist writing for the life section of the paper. Previously she had worked in Washington, covering politics, and Niels discovered an online article about an affair she had with a married congressman that led to her losing her job at a major news magazine. He dug deeper and discovered pictures. She had dark hair and a pale white face that was in contrast to a thick coating of ruby-red lipstick. She was pretty in a pasty, witchy sort of way. There was an aura of snobbish superiority in her pictures of one educated at a private girl's college on the East Coast.

She was a bit of a social butterfly who attended many of the movie industry galas and events. Niels would bide his time. He expected a savage article to come from her, but he remembered the old adage that all publicity was good publicity.

The article's headline read, "Upside-Down Grieving Widower's Fall from Grace." During the course of the interview, Madeline Dowdy interjected brief but devastating tidbits about Niels. The writing style was partly tongue-in-cheek and partly serious, siding with the women. Niels did admire the way the article flowed and how carefully she had designed her questions and the order she placed them to fit her objective to make Niels appear like a man in a serious midlife crisis. The ending read, "What possessed a successful insurance executive to throw away his career for a night of debauchery with a young staff member? Where will Niels Pettigrew be in five years?"

Niels took not one word of it to heart. Nor was he affected by it in the least. No, he was thrilled but needed to milk this for all it was worth.

He decided to e-mail Madeline Dowdy.

> Dear Ms. Dowdy,
>
> Thank you for your well-written and well-researched article. I do strongly disagree with some of your analysis and have a proposal to make to you. Debate me at the venue of your choice. The bigger, the better.
>
> Respectfully yours,
> Niels Pettigrew

Niels then posted on his blog and Facebook the interview and his challenge. He also arranged to have it posted on the radical women's blog.

Then came something unexpected, a request from a literary agent based in LA who had previously rejected his manuscript. Or more exactly an assistant had sent Niels the rejection informing him once again that her boss hadn't loved it enough. Oh, how he had learned to detest that phrase "I just didn't love it enough" or other variations, such as "I need to fall in love with a story before I can commit all my energies to such an undertaking."

> Dear Niels,
>
> After taking another look at your query letter and excerpt, at your convenience, please send me your manuscript *The Philanderer* as an attachment. I very much look forward to reading it.
>
> Sincerely,
> Cynthia Garvin
> Garvin Literary Agency

Niels had a sense that she had read his interview with Madeline Dowdy and that *love* was a fluctuating concept in the publishing industry.

Chapter 17

Madeline Dowdy needed little prompting. She immediately agreed to the debate and arranged for it to be held at a small liberal arts college in Northern California. It wasn't the big venue Niels had hoped for to attract literary agents, but it was a start. It could lead to bigger things. Niels knew the deck was being stacked against him, but if this would help him get published, so be it.

The format included three panelists who would ask questions and a moderator. Two weeks ahead of time, Niels was given the panelist names, and he went online to research. The first was a gay feminist law professor named Sarah Nystrom who had been involved in women's equality for decades. She had written a student guide on feminism and led a protest rally for women's rights on campus back in the seventies that included bra burnings. Second was Tim Freyman, an author whose last book dealt with the effects of the sixty's sexual revolution on today's mores. Lonny Flanders, the third, was a publisher of a major and raunchy adult magazine. Niels took neither of the two men for granted as if they would be on his side. He considered pondering what question they might ask, but then he thought again. Don't clog your mind with data. Let them fire away. Stay calm, and no matter what, don't let them see you sweat.

Two days before the debate, Niels flew to San Francisco. He rented a car and drove up the coast. Then he headed inland through a coniferous forest with predominantly tall evergreens. As he was driving through the woodland, he spotted a red-tailed hawk and a northern flicker. Farther on, the land changed to rolling hills with small farms dotting the landscape. When Niels heard a honking cacophony overhead, he pulled over next to a meadow and observed a V formation of Canadian geese soaring across a blue sky.

On his way back to the car, he spotted what he thought at first was a shrike on a tree stump. But something told him to stop dead in his tracks and look again. He focused his binoculars, and he saw that it was the size of a shrike with similar gray upper parts but that it had a black face mask and black wings. This was no shrike but a northern wheatear, a rare bird and a first for Niels. What a thrill.

This passerine bird had a great migration range from its winter base in Northern Africa that included Eurasia and Greenland and Canada. The camera was in the car, but he needed to keep his entire body still, even his breath so that he would not to startle the bird that was less than thirty feet away.

Scanning the thin dry grass below for insects, it swooped down, scampered about, pecking the ground. It flew back to its perch atop the stump with a fat spider in its slender beak.

Niels remained still as the bird scanned the area for predators. No hawks or other birds of prey in sight, it dropped its meal, and in a swift series of pecks and scans, the spider was quickly eaten.

"Chack-chack, dweet," the little bird chirped before it flew off. Niels watched until it disappeared over a line of trees in the distance.

Here he was across the country en route to a debate to promote his manuscript, and out of the blue, he had a special moment birding. Another unlikely conjunction of events had occurred in Niels's life that he had no control over. Or was there something more? In his pursuit for one goal—a published manuscript—did other opportunities arrive as a by-product?

By dusk, Niels arrived in Cascade Falls, which lay at the foot of the Klamath Mountains, a beautiful expanse of white peaks in the gloamy distance. The place had a gritty college-town atmosphere with a couple of dive bars and a pizza and sub shop sprinkled along the main street.

Niels had reservations at a B and B in town and within walking distance of the campus. After checking in to his spare but quaint room on the second floor with a view of the mountains, Niels went to a local restaurant for dinner, and then, tired after a long day of travel, turned in early.

After breakfast at his B and B, Niels drove out to a nearby national park and parked at the foot of the mountains for a day of birding. At the park's entrance gate, he was greeted by a park ranger in a booth. Niels had forgotten to renew his annual pass, and he paid five dollars to enter.

In the past this would have aggravated him to no end—first that he had not renewed and second that he had to pay money to view wildlife in the first place. What would John Muir have thought? Walking and hiking about this country's great woodlands and forests should be free. But he handed the ranger a five-dollar bill and parked in a gravel lot.

There were a few cars, but Niels saw not one person about. At the trailhead there was a bulletin board with a map of the park and folded maps in a plastic sleeve. Niels put one in his back pocket and studied the big map for a moment. He saw where the lake was, and then he entered a wide trail into the forest.

In his research Niels had discovered that this area's geology was endemic to a variety of cedar and pine trees. It was like a cathedral of tall trees with little undergrowth, the forest floor littered in pine needles and scalelike foliage, an aura of serenity in the air.

The trail meandered through the woods until it came to an open area with picnic tables and a log cabin restroom.

Farther up, Niels came to the edge of the lake. He went off the trail and walked along the water's perimeter until he came to a small meadow with a rainbow collection of wildflowers. A flock of geese were floating in the water. Then one flapped its wings and skittered across the water, its feet barely touching the surface. Another followed suit, and then another went. It looked as if they were walking on water. What a sight! Niels didn't even need his binoculars. They were no more than thirty feet away.

Back on the trail, he came to a tiered outcrop of granite carved by Mother Nature into a hillside. He climbed up to a level area of rock, took off his hiking belt, and sat with his back against a rock wall. He swept the area with his binoculars.

He heard a *ho-ho-hoo-hoo hoot* followed by a low *whoo-oo* coming from a cluster of trees. He adjusted his lens to focus in and waited. Again there was a hoot, and Niels looked to his left. He heard another hoot, and there it was, perched high in a tall oak—a great horned owl.

How out of place the oak tree appeared with its green leafy foliage surrounded by bristly pine. The bird had one foot higher on the branch that jutted out at an angle from the trunk, but that was no matter. The owl had adjusted its legs to the situation and seemed comfortable with its body parallel to the tree.

The owl leaned its head forward, its oval eyes with yellow irises and round black pupils looking into the lens and seeming to be saying, "Do you belong here?" A shiver ran through Niels as he looked into those wild, inquiring eyes before the owl looked away.

It was a magnificent specimen of the Strigiformes order, a big owl with a white patch on the throat. Its underparts were light brown and flecked white. How strange and beautiful this solitary creature appeared with its hornlike ears and round gray face. Like the surrounding land, there was an aura of serenity about this nighttime predator.

With a flap of its wings, it leaped down on another branch perpendicular to the trunk. It got itself situated and then straightened its legs, leaning itself forward while its wings drew out and back.

What a treat! First the geese walking on water and now an owl stretching. It appeared quite comfortable in this habitat, familiar to the land and waters, a strong, healthy bird. Then it was gone, flying over the formation of rocks and then out of sight.

Like yesterday, it was another rewarding days birding, not in numbers but in the rarity and specialness of the moments.

And what led him here began with the occurrence of a meteorological phenomenon—wind shear. That had also led to the death of his wife, which got the ball rolling. He had flown to Spain and met another phenomenon, Nina. He had discovered his writing muse while he was over there. He had returned home and begun a fitness regimen and a philanderer's lifestyle that was at the core of his manuscript. All that had resulted in him being here in this forest and this great day of birding.

Back in town Niels walked over to the college. The school was on ten acres with four residence halls, a library, a gymnasium, and the centerpiece—the liberal arts center—where the debate would take place. Brick pathways divided the college green into four sectors, each with semicircular stone benches on a raised brick patio.

Niels took a seat facing the liberal arts center adorned with spiraled roof-cap turrets stationed at each corner, Gothic arch windows, and dormers running the length of the roofs.

He walked over and read a placard at the entrance. Niels couldn't believe it. The building was named after John Muir, Muir Hall. It was built in 1869 by a timber tycoon as a mansion. In 1910, the family heirs donated the property to a private group of environmentalists who built the college.

Off the main lobby was an alcove with a bust of Muir, and on the wall hung pictures of the environmentalist during various stages of his career. One that struck Niels was of Muir and President Teddy Roosevelt at Yosemite, the older Muir with his scraggly beard and the robust president standing in front of a giant redwood. Even from the grainy photo, there was a glint of moral righteousness about these two great men. What would they think of this farce of a debate Niels was entangled in, all to get a damn book published.

He told himself he that didn't regret his conduct since his wife's passing or what he was about to engage in tomorrow. He had to believe it, for he needed to give a strong performance at the debate in the hopes of drawing attention to his manuscript.

It was deep in his core that he was a writer, and a published manuscript would validate him as such. Writing a good story was not enough. He needed others to read it and confirm that he was, indeed, a writer. And if he needed to play a part for a bit longer, he would do so.

The remainder of the building housed a conference center, offices for staff, and of course, the auditorium, where Niels now stood. A sense of foreboding came over Niels as again his conscience trickled out the thought of the fool he would be making of himself. What would his daughter think? And what would Laura think if she were still alive? "Balderdash," Niels muttered under his breath as he wondered if the influence of Muir on this campus was somehow infiltrating his subconscious. He told himself not to overthink it as he left the building.

At a local restaurant he had prime rib for dinner, which was excellent, and then he wrote in his journal before turning in for the evening.

> NP spotted a northern wheatear on the way to the college, an unforgettable moment. Then he followed that up with a grand day of birding at a national park. Birding mattered to him. It had always mattered.
>
> Here he was on his way to debate a philanderer's effect on women, and en route, he spots a rare bird. That alone had made the trip worthwhile. Then he discovered that John Muir had a hall named after him at the college. He sensed that the synchronicity

> of events on this trip—the great day of birding, the Muir Hall, the debate where he would defend philandering—was nearing a point where the dust would settle and NP would find his true path. Through all that had transpired since his wife's death, birding had remained a constant, his one constant.
>
> This led NP to introspection on the vagaries of life as the events going on around him were coalescing toward a revelatory moment.

At three the next afternoon, Niels came up to a line waiting outside the auditorium. He showed his ID and was escorted past the students, some pointing and talking in hush tones as he went by. "That's him," one girl blurted out.

Cable lines ran everywhere as a camera crew set up below the stage where there were two lecterns facing a rectangular-shaped table with three chairs. Niels approached a woman dressed in dark slacks and a white blouse who seemed to be in charge. "Excuse me. I'm Niels Pettigrew."

The woman whirled around. "Ah, Mr. Pettigrew," she said as she sized up Niels, "Jean Breskin here." She was a slender woman in her late thirties with a mop of frizzy hair and delicate facial features with large, intelligent eyes. She had feminist intellectual written all over her.

She offered a hand toward the stage. "If you would be so kind as to go backstage for makeup."

"And you would be?" Niels said sharply. He was a bit on edge as a conflict raged in his mind about the spectacle he was about to enter. He reminded himself that all publicity was good publicity, but the moment had a grip on him. Maybe he really was a macho pig, for this woman had set off alarm bells that he was in enemy territory.

Breskin handed Niels a business card. "I'm with the local public television station." She ran her finger along the bottom of her lip, her browed furrowed. "Is there a problem?"

Niels looked up from the card listing Jean Breskin in raised ink as *Director of Public Affairs, Northern California.* "No one told me anything about television, public television, no less."

"I see," Breskin tilted her head to the side, her eyes studying Niels. "Would you like to call it off?" Her tone said, "Go ahead. See if I give a damn."

Pull yourself together, Niels told himself. He needed to summon his philandering beast that rolled with the punches life offered up. "Absolutely not," he said as his nerves steadied, and once again he was ready to take on all comers. "Just one thing."

"Yes."

"Anymore surprises you and your cohorts have in store for me?"

Breskin blinked her eyes once and then again as if she couldn't believe what she had heard. "Yes, if this goes well, it will be aired at a later date across the nation on PBS."

"Really?"

"Yes, Mr. Pettigrew, really."

There were two mirrors backstage at the far end along a wall, and two men with the backs of their heads to Niels were already getting made up. From the mirror's reflections, Niels recognized Lonny Flanders and Tim Freyman. They were talking as two women worked on applying powder to their faces.

They got up and headed back for the stage. Tim Freyman walked past Niels, but Flanders stopped. "I'll bet you're Pettigrew," Flanders said in a big voice that had a ring of merriment to it.

Niels nodded. "That's me."

"Love your blog. Loooovee it," Flanders hooted.

Lonny Flanders was a short fireplug of man with a tangle of red hair atop a large head. He had the look of a self-made, affluent redneck who as a kid always got into one scrap after another with authority figures.

"Thank you."

"Mr. Pettigrew," one of the makeup woman said, "Need to get you done."

Flanders slapped Niels on the shoulder. "Go on, boy. Get her done."

As Niels started his makeup, he saw through the mirror a woman approaching. Madeline Dowdy looked older in person than her pictures had indicated. Her face wasn't particularly wrinkled, but it seemed in need of sunshine and fun. She appeared part sexy vamp with her heavy massacre and bright red lipstick and part dowager with her tired eyes and pallid skin. Madeline sat next to Niels and looked at him in the mirror. "Well, well—"

Niels cut in, "Said the spider to the fly." He smiled in the mirror and received a thin, sly grin in return.

"Touché," Madeline said. "Niels Pettigrew, I presume."

Niels caught her checking him over a tic too long. It was a look he had come to know, a look he hoped to use to his advantage. "Madeline Dowdy, be gentle with me tonight. I am a fragile, misguided soul." His philanderer side had taken over.

The two makeup women gagged to fight the laughter dying to erupt from their mouths. Both paused for a moment, looked at each other, smiled, and went back to dabbing cotton swabs of powder on his forehead.

"My motto in a debate is shoot the wounded and take no prisoners," Madeline said through a neat little smile.

"I gathered that from the piece you did on me." Niels looked at her in the mirror. Their eyes locked for a moment, and in her gaze there was a glimmer of amusement.

She offered a thin, coy smile to the mirror. "Let us save the repartee for the debate."

* * *

The moderator, a professor at the college, was dressed in a dark suit and bow tie with the erudite air of pedantry.

He explained that each panelist would ask a question and then would have a follow-up with five minutes of give-and-take. They would go four rounds. Then each debater would have a closing statement.

Sarah Nystrom went first. "Since we are here at a college that is greatly influenced by the teachings of John Muir, I have a quotation of his. 'The gross heathenism of civilization has generally destroyed nature, and poetry, and all that is spiritual.'" She folded her hands on the desk and said, "Isn't that exactly what your blog is doing, Mr. Pettigrew?" The PA system let out a loud droning shriek. Professor Nystrom made a face to indicate her displeasure and leaned back as a tech came up to her mic and made an adjustment. "As I was saying," Nystrom said, "aren't you destroying all that is spiritual with your hedonistic rants?"

"Here's another quote by John Muir," Niels said with both hands firmly gripping the edges of the lectern. "'The mountains are calling, and I must go.'"

"I am not talking about mountains, Mr. Pettigrew."

"Neither am I, madam," Niels said as he raised and lowered his eyebrows like Groucho Marx. "Neither am I."

A stir of muted laughter came from the audience.

"I would like to quote some of your quips to your readers, Mr. Pettigrew." The professor looked up at Niels and then at a sheet of paper on her table. "In the art of seducing a woman, one must know how to close the deal." She looked up, the corner of her mouth twisted in a scowl. "You think of a woman as something to be conquered, not as an equal." She stared at Niels, demanding an answer.

"I think of woman as having something I want. I don't approach them under any false pretense." Niels raised his arms out to the side. "What is wrong with sex, Professor Nystrom? Would you have the same problem when a woman acts in a similar manner?"

"Another quote," Sarah said, ignoring his question. "We're men. We have an itch that's wired to think about sex every fifteen seconds. So let's scratch that itch." Sarah grimaced, revealing a row of small teeth that brought to mind an angry rodent. "Mr. Pettigrew, do you really think all men think about sex all the time?"

"Hah," Niels said through a victory smile. "You don't know men, do you, Professor?"

Sarah Nystrom started to speak, but Niels raised his hand and continued, "I approach women with no pretense. They know who I am and what I want. They have the right to say no." Niels shrugged. "What is it about a blog that offers advice that bothers you so?"

"Everything," Sarah spat out. "But wouldn't you agree, Mr. Pettigrew, that some men have used your advice to scam women under the pretext of love and have done irreparable harm to unsuspecting women."

"People can take any type of advice and twist it to suit their sordid ways."

"Answer the question." Sarah leaned forward, folded hands brought under her chin. "Has your advice been used in a harmful manner?"

"Not to my knowledge." Niels straightened his shoulders and started to cross his arms across his chest before he caught himself. *Don't let them see you sweat.* "Why do you deny the biological fact that men are different from women?"

Nystrom shook her head at Niels, her eyes squinting with contempt. She turned to Madeline. "Ms. Dowdy, what do you find most offensive about Mr. Pettigrew's blog?" She paused for a moment and checked her notes. "Musings of a Philanderer?"

Madeline nodded as if she was considering something of great consequence. "Everything about it, including the title." She glanced at Niels, who smiled back. She continued in an even, emotionless voice. "The definition of a philanderer is a dissolute person." She shot a sharp-eyed glance at Niels and held it. "A man who is morally unrestrained." She turned back to face the panel. "If I may read a few of his more disturbing words of wisdom. 'A woman showing cleavage is like a flashing neon sign reading open for business down below.'" Madeline paused and looked up for a moment, her expression saying, "This guy doesn't get it." "Here's another. 'Every woman wants it whether she knows it or not. It's up to you to convince her.'"

Madeline sighed with heavy, dramatic flair. "This man makes a mockery out of everything women have fought to attain for more than a century. He thinks he is a harmless rogue," she said as she tipped her head toward Niels. "But his blog represents women as not equal or even human." She turned and faced Niels and said, "But as something to be conquered and done away with as nothing more than used up garbage." She put a special upper-crust East Coast twist on the second syllable of *garbage.*

A roar of applause and shouts erupted from the audience. Some young women stood, fists pumping.

She's good, Niels thought as the moderator asked the audience to behave and then told Lonny Flanders it was his turn.

"Ms. Dowdy," Lonny said, lowering his gaze over his eyeglasses, "exactly what is wrong with a blog giving young men advice on getting laid?"

The moderator interrupted, "Please, Mr. Flanders, let us keep some semblance of civility."

Flanders shrugged indifferently, his gaze on Madeline. "Well?"

"Mr. Flanders," she said with a particular tone of scorn, "why do you and your ilk look at women as only an object for the procurement of sex?"

"I—"

Madeline cut him off, "I have not finished my thought." She narrowed a challenging gaze on Flanders. "Instead of us as an equal." She jabbed her finger at Flanders, her expression animated but under control. "Your magazine degrades women. It makes them something less than human." She paused for effect like a preacher on a good roll. "You and he," she said as she jerked her thumb in Niels's direction, "are a detriment to feminism."

Another uproar of approval came from the audience.

Flanders flashed his "good ole boy" smile. "Mr. Pettigrew," he said with a twinkle of derring-do in his eyes, "what's the best advice you can give any of the young fellas here in attendance on closing the deal?"

Sarah Nystrom stood. "I won't stand for this." She turned to the moderator and said, "If this is going to be some frat boy debate, then I am leaving."

The moderator raised his hands, but before he could speak, Flanders said, "Can't stand the heat, darlin', I suggest you get out of the kitchen." Niels thought that Flanders and Leia Childs would have gotten along fabulously.

Sarah turned and faced her tormentor with clenched fists as if ready to strike. She was a square block of a woman with short-cropped hair, a high forehead stamped on a pugnacious face, a bulldog ready to break loose from the chain.

Niels glanced over at Madeline, a thin smile on her face of one enjoying herself. She was a character playing a role, no more. He wondered if she even believed what she had said. And then he thought about how similar it was to his performance. *Stay in character,* Niels told himself as he looked at the combative Sarah. *She's definitely a true believer,* he thought as she stared at Flanders, her eyes two withering slits.

Flanders raised his hands, a modicum of respect in his gaze. *Might this irate woman strike me?* "All right. Settle down." He turned to the moderator, "If I might continue."

And so it went with more give-and-take until it was Tim Freyman's turn. He began a long-winded question for Madeline about the historical significance of woman's liberation as a springboard for other suppressed groups. It was as though all the air had left the room. But Madeline gave a stirring answer with an impressive knowledge of American history with specific references to unions fighting for workers' rights, civil rights, and *Roe v. Wade.*

Niels then stated that he was for equal rights for every person, but he didn't see the connection between these just causes and his blog. "Your knowledge of American history is very impressive, Ms. Dowdy," Niels said as he leaned his head toward her, but he kept his eyes on the camera. "But your juxtaposition to my blog is at the very least disingenuous."

After the panel had completed their rounds of questions and answers—Niels thought it was a draw—they each had five minutes to speak.

Madeline peppered her closing comments with such phrases as *myopic view of women, exploiters of the female form into a fantasy world of debauchery, bottom-feeders.* Her tone was reasonable, her expression placid, and she was a master at stringing words together to hold the audience's attention.

Niels thanked the college, the students for coming, and the panel and moderator. He didn't want to take five minutes. He wanted to make one point and then end it with a sales pitch.

He stated that he found Madeline Dowdy an excellent speaker, but he thought her words were empty. "People have a right to choose whether they want to read my blog or not, if they so choose." He raised his hands, palms out, "The big news I would like to share this evening." He took a moment and made contact with the camera and then the audience. No one had left, and he had their undivided attention. "I have written a *fictional* memoir titled—" He offered his hand toward Flanders. "Sir, might you guess the name?"

A big smile spread the ruddy, lived-in face of the publisher. "*The Philanderer*," he said in an exaggerated voice as if he was introducing something of great importance.

Niels beamed a smile and pointed. "Exactly." He extended his hands in front of himself and out toward the camera. "If any publishers or literary agents out there are looking for the next big seller, contact me, Niels Pettigrew."

Afterward, Niels ran into Flanders and Madeline behind the stage, chatting and laughing like old friends. "Do you two know each other?"

"Hah," Flanders bellowed, "we've been going at it for years."

Madeline's face showed little emotion. "I believe strongly in equality for women." She shrugged and squinted at Niels. "The rest is just for show."

Flanders excused himself, leaving the two combatants alone.

"You write well. You'll be getting calls on your manuscript after this airs nationally," Madeline said.

"You think so?"

"I used to write book reviews back in DC. There's one thing I learned about the publishing industry," she said, raising a finger. "Make that two things. Sex sells, and an author involved in a controversy about sex sells even better."

"Do you have time to get a drink," Niels said. "There's something I would like to discuss with you."

* * *

"Let's just say I know and have met your type." Madeline tapped her hand on the bar and ordered. After Niels ordered, she turned to him. "I've learned the hard way not to mix business with pleasure."

The bartender returned with a gimlet—Madeline had instructed that it was vodka and lime juice—and a draft beer.

"Ah, one or the other," Niels said as he scanned the empty room, save a couple of old boys down at the far end. The place was a dive with a requisite mirror and bottles of liquor behind the bar. Everything about this joint was cheap, including the rickety booths and the peeling linoleum floor. In a couple of hours, it most likely would be filled with students, some probably discussing the debate.

Niels had only asked if she would consider looking at his manuscript, but she was on to him. Something in the way he had looked at her had given him away, something he had wanted to give away. He thought she might like the attention, and if necessary, he would end up in the sack with her. If not, no problem. Whatever it took to assist in publication. The swift and ruthless nature of his analysis had surprised him, but there it was.

"Well?" Madeline said between sips of her gimlet.

"Is there a time limit?"

Madeline removed the lime from her drink and sucked out its juices. "Do you know that a gimlet was used as a double entendre by Hemingway in a short story?"

"Really?" Niels had read the story and learned it in his study of Hemingway, but he didn't want to ruin her moment.

"Uh-huh," Madeline said as she raised her glass. "Marta Macomber, one of my favorite characters had a line I never forgot. 'I'll have a gimlet too. I need something.'" She took a sip and looked at Niels to see if he understood.

"I get it," he said through an acknowledging smile. "A small hand tool used for boring holes."

A pleased expression came over her face. "Very good."

"Well," Niels said as he put down his beer and wiped his mouth with his finger. "I need something too." He nodded his head as if he was trying to convince himself. "I'll take the edit." He put his hand on hers and said, "Afterward, maybe we could share a gimlet."

> NP thought the debate was entertaining, and he had put all he had into it. But afterward, before he retired for the night, he thought himself a fool, a grown man acting like some college prankster. But he was pragmatic enough to know that sometimes, to reach a goal, one had to do things that they were no longer comfortable with, such as trying to pick up his opponent in the debate. He felt as though, while he was talking with her about his manuscript, he needed to stay in his character, the philanderer.

And at this point in his life, that was what it had come down to—NP playing a role.

He remembered Nina's comment about looking forward, always look forward. But she didn't always look forward, for in her art she looked to the past. And then it came over NP that he looked to the past in his art—writing—searching for answers and explanations for his actions as he went forward in stops and starts in the present world. When he figured out his final destination, he would have the real new beginning in this life.

Chapter 18

After his daily five-mile morning walk, Niels took a shower and went downstairs to his writing room. The former dining room now made clear what Niels's two passions were.

Stacks of literary magazines and novels littered with Post-it tags where Niels had highlighted prose spilled out of an open wooden cabinet. Next to his *American Heritage Dictionary* on his desk was a quotation framed and in large bold print by Samuel Beckett. "Ever tried. Ever failed. No matter. Try again. Fail again. Fail better."

A picture Niels had taken at Ebro Delta of the dancing flamingos was framed and hanging on the wall along with pictures of songbirds and a print of an ivory-billed woodpecker in flight over a swamp.

Niels always stared at his ivory-billed woodpecker before he started writing, gaining inspiration from this uniquely magnificent creature with its triangular head with a red crest. A streak of white ran down the extended neck, crossed the black body, and then merged with an edge of white on the glossy black wings. It was the biggest of the woodpecker family with a thirty-inch wingspan, and many had considered it extinct for decades until a rash of controversial sightings in the last few years. The Lord God Bird may be not dead after all.

He had two e-mails in the in-box. The first was a second rejection letter from the LA agent.

Dear Niels,

I am very glad to have had the opportunity to consider your work, but in the end I just didn't fall in love with it in the ways I need to in order to offer representation. I wish you the best of luck in finding a home for *The Philanderer.*

Sincerely,
Cynthia Garvin
Garvin Literary Agency

Sons of bitches! Who are these people? Niels wondered if Madeline's newspaper interview didn't provide enough of a buzz. But deep down he knew that the story wasn't there yet.

The second e-mail—which confirmed his realization that the story wasn't finished—was Madeline's edit of his manuscript on an attachment with a two-page critique in the body. She found the manuscript well written and holding her interest "with potential for a big seller," but she was unsatisfied with the beginning and the ending. "Shorten the beginning and get him on the airplane with Nina. That's where the story begins. Give the reader a glimpse of who he was before he flies overseas and show how his world has been turned upside down. Possibly the scene at his wife's funeral and one or two afterward in his environment. But get him on that plane ASAP! Also, he is not developed enough for the readers to get a grip as to why the sudden change in character from John Boy Walton to Charlie Sheen."

Further on in her critique, she wrote. "The protagonist must come to some sort of resolution as to who he once was and who he is at end of story and what he had learned. Watching a woman driven off in a limo doesn't get it. He and the conclusion comes across as incomplete." She ended with, "The middle of the story is a bawdy, engaging romp, but the beginning and end need work. Figure out who NP is, and you'll have it." Much of what she had suggested was Leia's advice. *Indeed,* Niels thought. *Indeed.*

On page one, Niels began his rewrite.

> Over a rise at the far end of the cemetery, a line of trees flushed in brilliant hues of red and gold met an azure horizon with stunning clarity. The squeaky iterations of a wren rising in volume and pitch and ending in a rapid cascade of tweets caught NP's ear over the reverend's drone. "Laura, a generous contributor to church functions and projects, staunch member of MADD, dutiful Christian, and faithful wife and mother to—"
>
> *Balderdash,* NP thought. *She had another side that he was only too aware of.*

Writing had helped Niels understand the breadth of his wife's control over him—her disdain for alcohol and puritanical disapproval of anything suggesting the risqué in books, movies, or even their bedroom for that matter.

But should he interject something so personal into the story? The writer in him told him he must face the truth and write it as he saw it, as he felt it. Plus, it was fiction, wasn't it?

He needed to show the wife stilting his protagonist's life, not in great detail for fear of taking away from the story, but then he needed to reveal how her influence affected him while she was alive, how he changed after her death, and how he ended up at the conclusion. It was like putting together a giant jigsaw puzzle with amorphous parts that changed not only their shape but their position too.

He agreed with Madeline in that he must show something of who his character once was, but not too much. She was right. It might bore the reader. The real story was his escapades, his transformation, and the ending he had yet to write. Ah, the rub.

He remembered the old adage from writing class. *Show. Don't tell.* So he needed to show NP's vulnerability when he met the exotic Spanish woman on the plane. He was someone in a confused state who didn't understand that something had snapped in him, exposing a damaged man. He was a man who found relief from the sudden upheaval in his life by living in a world that was the polar opposite of what he had lived in before.

He needed to complete this as if he was looking at it as an outsider. He must disengage himself from his swell of sentiment from Madeline's succinct comments about Neal Pendry's mental state. Write with a perspective of distance like a good birder in a forest teeming with wildlife. He must see Neal Pendry with the same objective eye as the other characters, all the while knowing his biggest challenge was the ending.

After seven hours of grinding away, Niels had rewritten the opening chapter. It would need refining, but he was done working on the manuscript for the day.

Though his blog had an avid following, it hadn't drawn the attention of literary agents. He needed the debate to go nationally.

He had ignored the blog since he had returned home from California. He was mulling over whether to continue. He didn't have it in him anymore to write such raunchy fluff, and the readers were for the most part imbeciles. What would Professor Sarah Nystrom think?

He would not write the blog anymore. Something had changed. He was changing, always changing. It seemed he had been in a continual flux since the death of his wife. He wrote the following post: "After much consideration, I am closing down this site to devote all my energy to finishing my manuscript aptly titled *The Philanderer*." Niels thought about going further with a witty ditty but decided against it. It wasn't in him. The only thing in him now was finishing his story.

He notified his advertisers on the site. He received an immediate reply from Lonny Flanders asking him to reconsider and adding that he was considering Niels for a monthly column. Niels wrote back and thanked him but respectfully declined in order to concentrate on completing his manuscript. A couple of months ago, Niels would have jumped at the chance, but not now. Something was different since his return from Dallas, something he couldn't put his finger on. He was drifting away from his wolfish, womanizing ways, but to where he wasn't sure.

Flanders wrote back that he didn't really understand but added, "When you complete the book, let me know. I have connections with some major publishing houses. If your book is half as good as your blog—" That was great news, but he needed one more thing to come through as he removed a business card from his wallet and ran his finger over the name in raised ink.

He dialed the telephone number. After he was put on hold for five minutes by an aide, Jean Breskin answered.

"Hello, this is Niels Pettigrew, I debated Madeline—"

Jean cut in, "I remember. What can I do for you?"

"Any decision yet on airing the debate nationally?"

After a pause Jean said in an irritated tone. "Yes, the last Sunday of next month."

"Do you have a time?"

"Eight p.m. on the East Coast."

"Really?"

"Yes, really, if that's—"

He knew Jean was still peeved with the brusque manner he had treated the director before the debate. "I want to apologize for the manner I spoke to you before the debate. I thought I was getting ambushed."

"We don't do ambushes," Jean said evenly.

"Last question," he said. "No, make that two. How was the debate received in Northern California, and how did I do?"

"We received more local mail than any show since I've been directing, and you and Madeline Dowdy knocked it out of the park."

"Is that right?"

"In my opinion, after the national airing, your manuscript, if it's any good, will be in demand."

* * *

Niels awoke to the sound of morning thunder and heavy rain. Walking was out of the question. After a shower he dried himself in front of the mirror. His hair was now wavy and long, a thicket with a swirl of locks angled across his forehead. He dried the remainder of his body and took another look in the mirror. His hair bothered him. His rakish looks bothered him. He decided that he would get a haircut, not as short as before but something a bit more moderate.

He went to his writing room and his computer. The offer from Lonny Flanders to help with finding a publisher and Jean Breskin's glowing comments about the debate made it all the more imperative that Niels get this story in tip-top shape. He had six weeks until the debate would air nationally, and then he would wait and see.

He would hunker down to get the job done and keep contact with others limited, outside of birding on Saturdays. Of course, that should not be a problem since most contact socially had been initiated by Laura. She organized get-togethers with other couples, mostly from their church with an occasional gathering of birders. She arranged vacations and set up times for volunteer work for the two of them. In many ways, while they were married, he had been on automatic pilot.

Recently Niels had been thinking about when they first met. At the time she seemed perfect, an attractive, reserved young woman who took an interest in Niels's passion.

He could not remember ever having a cross word with her. But in her quiet, strong-willed way, she had steered him to live according to her rules—no alcohol, no R-rated movies or books, contributing member of their church, and volunteer work for those less fortunate. The last part Niels never had a problem with. But with the first three, it now seemed as though a big part of him felt cheated.

For the last twenty-five years, he had been playing a role for the approval of his wife. He would write it in his story, for he was a writer, and writers must venture outside their comfort zones. As Niels opened up his story, he chuckled to himself. He had definitely gone outside of his comfort zone.

It rained for most of the week, and Niels didn't walk. He was a man possessed, working from early morning until late afternoon until he couldn't think straight. He decided to put morning walks on hold until after the manuscript was finished. He also noticed in passing while he brushed his teeth in the morning that he was putting weight back on. The lean, hard body was softening around the edges, and a trace of fleshiness was returning to his cheeks and jowls. He was by no means overweight as before, but he no longer had the flat, hard belly and defined definition. At the moment, his appearance gave him little concern other than making time for a haircut.

By Saturday, it had finally stopped raining, and Niels was picking up Mary Shorter and her husband, John, to meet their fellow birders at the park where Niels and Mary had birded together and later ended up back at her place in bed.

John got in the front seat, and Mary got in back. They exchanged hellos, and then John said, "We have some great news to share." He looked at Niels, his expression that of a boy at a circus. "We're pregnant."

Niels did a quick calculation in his head. He hadn't been with Mary for more than six months, so he wasn't the father. Whew. "Congratulations."

"I'll be pushing seventy when the baby graduates high school." John turned to his wife. "At least one of us will still be young enough to not be mistaken for a grandparent." John let out a self-deprecating laugh and swung his arm over his seat and took her hand in his. "It's the best thing that has ever happened to us."

Niels came to a stop sign and looked at Mary in the mirror. There was a content, happy glow to her that he had never seen before. None of this would be taking place if he had agreed to let her move in with him and leave John. Now something like that would be the furthest thing from the mind of this mother-to-be.

They met three couples and a newcomer named Barbara Winston in the parking lot. Her hair was in a pageboy, short and sleek, and her round, smooth face had a wholesome beauty. But what drew Niels to her were her eyes—large brown orbs that were lovely and sad as though she had suffered a recent loss.

After John and Mary announced their good news and received the heartfelt congratulations, they broke up in two groups. Barbara and two of the couples decided to go along the river, and John, Mary, and the remaining couple walked up along the ridgeline.

"What about you, Niels?" John said, "River or ridgeline?"

Niels stole a glance at Barbara and thought there was a look that said, "I won't be upset if you come with us."

"River," Niels said. His choice was easy even if Barbara wasn't there. Something about Mary bothered him. Was it that she had moved on from Niels only to become pregnant by a husband she had recently wanted to leave? Or could it be her lack of morality in having had an affair with Niels no less. Or was he a tad jealous at her newfound joy that was plastered all over her face? He realized his ambiguity, but it didn't sway his feelings toward Mary.

Anyway, he was attracted to Barbara, not as a lustful predator but as a person who wanted to be in the company of this quiet woman. He had the strongest urge to put his arm around her shoulder and rescue her.

Niels's group walked along the path that bordered the water. There wasn't a bird in sight on the river, and the trees along the bank were silent—a slow beginning. One of the men said, "Isn't this where you and Mary saw the red-necked phalarope, Niels?"

"Yes, up a little farther, between that opening of trees."

They came to the spot and stopped. "It swam in a circle, dipping its beak in the water," Niels said, pointing. "No more than fifteen feet from where we stand."

"I've always wanted to see a red-necked phalarope," Barbara said. She turned to Niels. "That must have been a thrill."

After they had no luck along the river, they went into the woods. They walked double file with Barbara next to Niels, as they seemed to have gravitated to each other. The whacking of a woodpecker tapping into a tree for insects reverberated in the forest. "A good sign," Barbara whispered.

"Look," Niels said, pointing. He liked being in this woman's company.

High in a pine tree was a huge pileated woodpecker with a striking red crest banging away. "That's the second one I've seen with a headdress," Barbara said.

"First for me," Niels said, shaking his head. "All these years, a first."

They glanced at each other, and in her eyes he saw many things. One, she had been told of his wife's passing. Two, she was interested, but not with the instant sexual undercurrent that he had experienced of late, more a "let's get to know each other" vibe. And lastly, there was that hint of anguish—possibly a bad divorce or maybe a loss of spouse. Niels wondered if anyone had ever seen it in him.

As they watched the bird hammer away, Niels thought how similar it was to the supposedly extinct ivory-billed woodpecker. But the ivory-billed woodpecker was more unique. Its bill was longer and gleaming white in color, and it had a long, recurved crest of blackish jet.

The great American woodpecker was done in by the logging of river forests and could not adapt to the second-growth woodland like the pileated had.

But in the last few years in the northeast corner of Louisiana, there were rumors of echoes of its distinct squeaky nasal call and then a double knock or whack on wood. But there was no real proof other than eyewitnesses and one short glimpse on film. Some experts claimed the video was a pileated woodpecker and that the ivory-billed was extinct—case closed.

Like any good birder, Niels hoped there were still some around, but even if they were, would they soon be gone, never to be seen again except its toxicological likeness in museums? Niels saw a replicate of an ivory-billed once in a small family-run museum in Florida. It was a beautiful creature with such great size not normally associated with the woodpecker family. It was shiny blue-black with white markings on its neck and back, and its triangular head was dominated by a striking red crest that gave it the appearance of rarity. An unusual looking bird that only a lucky few people alive today had ever seen or claimed to have seen. For now, Niels would have to be satisfied with his print of the great bird in his writing room. But someday maybe he would spot a Lord God Bird. The moniker was supposed to have been based on an exclamation from an awed birder when he saw the bird. "Lord God, what a bird."

The opportunity to see what few people would ever witness was what drew Niels to birding, something unusual in nature with a haunting song or ritual like when he saw the red-necked phalarope. Moments like that made birding so special, and watching the pileated bedecked in its headdress with Barbara had some extra specialness to it, a man and a woman observing a wild creature in nature, a creature not seen every day. And from that experience a relationship may flourish, one that Niels thought would do him just fine at this point in his life.

They birded in the woods until noon and then met back up with their fellow birders for lunch. The other group had a great day spotting birds of prey, and they even witnessed a bald eagle snatch a fish from the river. Other than the big woodpecker, it had been an uneventful morning of birding for Niels. Though he and Barbara had only talked about birding and the people involved in it, there was an undeniable attraction that Niels did nothing to dissuade.

It was not in the words they spoke but in the way they looked at each other. At first it was appraising, and then they established a comfort level between them. She was a smart, keen-eyed birder whose company was good medicine for Niels. Barbara was a no-nonsense, pragmatic soul. A few months ago, he might not have had any interest in her. She didn't seem like the type for a fling, more like one of those women with whom you were meant to spend a lifetime. And a few months ago, she would have had no interest in the philandering Niels Pettigrew. It seemed to Niels that his life was taking a turn in a direction with an end in sight, a direction that he would have a say in.

Over lunch the group talked birds, while Niels and Barbara exchanged a look every so often. Niels wondered if Mary would take notice, but she was in her happy place, chatting away like some radiant songbird chirping its song for all to hear. It was as though her affair with Niels had never happened, erased from her mind.

Niels's group hiked up the windy trail to the ridgeline. Niels and Barbara decided to observe from a parapet of stone while the others climbed higher.

The sky was clear with only a few thin clouds in the distance, the meandering river cutting its way through the verdant land and hills in the distance. Geese flying in formation followed the river heading south, honking and squawking.

The sight of it held Niels as if he hadn't appreciated such a moment in some time. He remembered the sense of excitement he felt birding in Ebro Delta, his aha moments as though he was birding from a new perspective. Now he realized it was life, not birding, that he was perceiving differently.

"Clapper rail at two o'clock."

Niels snapped out of his daydream. Swooping down along the water, a bird with gray upper parts, white flanks, and a long bill landed on a short patch of sand with a reedy marsh to its rear. "Are you sure?" Niels said. "The clapper rail is not indigenous to these parts. Might it be a king rail?"

"They're darker," Barbara said, "and with a distinctive dark brown cap."

"You're right," Niels said as he focused his binoculars. "I don't ever recall seeing one this far inland."

"I've noticed a change in the migratory patterns." The bird waded into the water, pecking the surface for insects. "Some survive, and some perish."

Niels mind flashed to the very endangered ivory-billed as he looked over at Barbara from the corner of his eye. There was something pragmatic and analytical in her gaze but with a trace of compassion in the mouth that formed a small open circle as if she was thinking, *Oh, I hope this one makes it.*

On the ride home from birding, John said to Niels, "I think you have an admirer in Barbara."

"Oh," Niels said more as a question.

Mary piped in from the backseat, "Bad divorce last year. Husband left her for a younger woman, no children. The bastard."

Niels peeked at Mary in the rearview mirror, nary a trace of sarcasm or bitterness about her. He wondered if she even remembered wanting to leave her older husband for him.

"I enjoyed her company," Niels said as he turned off onto a highway ramp. "We didn't talk about anything other than birding." Niels paused as he came to a yield sign and accelerated onto the three-lane road. He glanced at John. "Do you know anything about her?"

John shrugged his shoulders and tilted his head back toward Mary, who was sitting behind him.

"Works for a world health organization, travels quite a bit, and has been interested in birding since college," Mary said.

"Well, there you go, Niels," John said, chuckling. "The perfect woman for a fellow birder." He swung his shoulder around and faced Mary. "Wouldn't you say so, honey?"

Chapter 19

Niels removed his glasses and rubbed his eyes. He had put in ten hours on the story and had reached the conclusion. His protagonist, NP, had followed Niels's path back toward reexamining his values, but he still didn't have an ending. He had written some scenes where he met a single woman birding, but he had no *special* moment when he turns a page into a newer and stronger life. He and his character were still in a nebulous transition period. Time was of the essence because the debate was airing tonight, and if things went as he hoped, offers to read his manuscript would soon arrive.

He pushed away from his desk, went into the bathroom, and splashed water on his face. Then he wiped it with a towel. He secured his glasses back on his nose. He had gotten a haircut, but it was not the bristly cut of old Niels but rather a moderate trim. He no longer wore his contacts, but rather he donned the sleek tortoiseshell glasses that he had purchased in Spain.

In the mirror he saw someone halfway between his old self and the fitness buff. The sleek, sharp features were gone, replaced by a semifit man of fifty with a full head of hair and a handsome face that was a little soft around the edges.

Niels had begun walking in the mornings again, and he had returned to a diet that allowed for an occasional pizza and a few beers in the evening. And he planned on returning to the gym when he finished the manuscript, which had better be soon.

He had edited and reedited his manuscript for grammar and structural errors, and he was confident that it was well written and error-free. Now all he needed was an ending, five pages or so that brought everything full circle.

It was right there, and he couldn't see it. But it occurred to him that he would have to experience it first and then write it. Maybe it would happen after he watched the debate. He went downstairs and turned on the TV.

The moderator introduced the panelist, Sarah Nystrom, the gay professor who had been adversarial toward Niels, Lonny Flanders, and Tim Freyman, the nonfiction author. Madeline Dowdy was introduced, and then the camera went to Niels Pettigrew. The first thing that struck Niels was the contemptuous look on his face. It was a handsome face, no doubt, with sharply defined features and wavy hair, but his eyes were that of a child on some big adventure, immature eyes that seemed to take the proceedings as some romp in the park. *My God*, he thought, *was that me or me in character?*

Niels told himself to keep a distance in assessing the debate like a good birder. He sensed he might not like parts of the following hour, but still he had enough pragmatism to know that his former self could perform a service that his present state could not—get his manuscript published.

Niels Pettigrew's answers were confident and assured as he exchanged words with Professor Nystrom. He more than held his own and even maintained a calm demeanor as she grew more agitated with his answers. It was almost as if Niels was witnessing this for the first time. And in a way, he was, for when he had been in the heat of the moment, it had taken a great effort to stay in character as a calm, carefree philanderer whose smugness Niels did not care for anymore.

But he could not deny the overall appeal of the give-and-take between him and Madeline, and the panel, especially when Niels went at it with Sarah Nystrom and Madeline with Lonny Flanders, people at opposite poles debating the most appealing of subjects.

"Sex sells," Lonny Flanders retorted to Madeline. "And so do AK-47s," Madeline said with a wave of her hand at Flanders as if she were tossing away trash.

Niels was fascinated as he watched, transfixed. The Niels Pettigrew before him seemed not like a stranger but someone or something that he had evolved from, a man who had gone from one extreme so far that he fell off course. Only now was he finding his true path.

Through it all he kept his focus on finding an ending to the story, searching for some conclusion that made sense of all that he had been through and taken him forward.

After the show was over, Niels sat staring at his TV as the credits rolled on the screen. "Production director, Jean Breskin" caught his eye. Niels remembered his phone call to Jean and her response that he and Madeline had "knocked it out of the park." And he had to admit that yes, it was an entertaining show.

He turned off the television and got out the book on Muir, which he had finally finished reading one evening after dinner. It had provided some reconnection with the great man. He leafed through it, scanning the pages until he came to a quote by Muir. "A natural inherited wildness in our blood." Could it be that his wildness had been misdirected in his philandering and that he would soon be able to redirect it toward the great outdoors and Barbara—a new and better version of a twofer? Could he find his salvation in a woman who, like him, had lost a mate—and in nature, as Muir had?

The morning after, Niels took a long walk and then went to his computer. To his surprise, he had ten requests from literary agents for his entire manuscript and three from publishers he hadn't even queried. One was from the LA agent, Cynthia Garvin, who had rejected him twice. She wrote of her many contacts with the big publishing houses and how she knew she could find a good home for his story. Never once did she explain her sudden newfound interest. Sons of bitches! Now the shoe was on the other foot.

Niels began typing.

> Dear Cynthia,
>
> I am very glad to have had the opportunity to consider your offer of representation, but in the end, I did not fall in love with it in the ways I need to in order to go forward in publishing *The Philanderer.* I wish you the best of luck in your future endeavors.
>
> Regards,
> Niels Pettigrew

Niels clicked the send button and began laughing in great guffaws. The irony of this moment was too sweet. Yes, he knew he should have been a bigger person and not done something so petty, but by golly, it felt so good to return a bit of their own medicine. Sons of bitches, indeed.

Niels picked up the phone and dialed. A woman's voice answered on the other end. "Barbara, Niels here. How are things going on the left coast?"

"Niels," she said in a pleasant tone of surprise, "just finishing up a report, and I am heading home tomorrow morning. Can't wait to bird this weekend."

"Me too. Afterward, would you like to have dinner at my place?"

"Niels, that sounds great."

After he hung up, he turned to his computer. He had his ending.

> NP's only diversion from writing had been Saturdays birding, and Betty had attended three out of five, always making sure he knew when she

wouldn't be there the next week because of business travel. They hadn't gone out on a date yet, but there seemed a tacit understanding that they had something between them, something that Betty didn't seem to want to rush. She had mentioned to NP the devastating effects the divorce had had on her. She barely ate or slept for weeks on end, and she had gone through the motions at work.

In the last few months, she had pulled herself out of it. So he went slow and easy with her, and in her gaze there was a gleam of appreciation, a look that said, "Thank you for understanding, and if you give me a little time, I would very much like to spend time with you." All that in a look, a look that before his writing career, NP would have never noticed. Maybe even in the beginning he might have missed it. But not now, for he was in complete writer's mode—observing, taking notes, examining his inner self and the world around him. How fascinating and rewarding it was to discover things about oneself and the world through the creativity of the human mind.

Last week, on the perimeter of a meadow flush with quail underfoot, NP had told Betty how he used to travel for business and what a grind it became. She told him, "When I was younger, I enjoyed the travel, but it has gotten old." She looked off for a moment and then back as the volley of bobwhites ricocheted in the meadow. "And once I got married, I couldn't wait to get home, and then later when my husband left—" Her voice trailed off before she pointed to a bird flying upward from the cover of the tall grass, two black bands on its white breast glistening in the early light of morning.

"Kildeer at eleven o'clock," she said as she raised her binoculars and watched the bird fly away.

"I know what you mean," NP said as he adjusted his lens on a line of trees at the meadow's edge. "Once I was living alone, everything changed for me. I changed." Another round of bobwhites whistled back and forth. "It seems it has taken over a year for me to get my bearings back." He brought his field glasses down and turned to her. "But not as who I used to be or was even three months ago, but the person I am now." NP paused and looked at her, really looked at her. "Do you know what I mean?"

Without missing a beat, Betty said, "Yes, I know."

She looked at NP with such utter compassion and understanding. Nina's saying about the eyes being the mirrors to the soul flashed through his mind. "You know what, Betty," NP said, "we're good together."